SO-CGP-871

ALASKAN MAGIC

ALASKAN MAGIC

•

Theresa Goldstrand

AVALON BOOKS
THOMAS BOUREGY AND COMPANY, INC.
401 LAFAYETTE STREET
NEW YORK, NEW YORK 10003

c.1

© Copyright 1998 by Theresa Goldstrand
Library of Congress Catalog Card Number: 98-96613
ISBN 0-8034-9324-X
All rights reserved.
All the characters in this book are fictitious,
and any resemblance to actual persons,
living or dead, is purely coincidental.

PRINTED IN THE UNITED STATES OF AMERICA
ON ACID-FREE PAPER
BY HADDON CRAFTSMEN, BLOOMSBURG, PENNSYLVANIA

Dedicated to the maverick son who inspired an Alaskan fantasy.

I wish to thank John Wren, Jack Libby, Robert Gamble, and Joseph Bork for their technical advice and assistance.

Chapter One

"Hey, be careful."

"Wanna do this yourself? I could be back in town havin' a cold one."

"Just clip the transmitter wire—not the receiver."

"Listen, I know what I'm doing. Hold that light still so we can get out of here."

The accomplice strained to listen for any sound that would detect intrusion into their project.

"It's done. Let's go." The man stood and warily looked about. "Come on."

The pair cautiously eased over the bow of the deserted fishing vessel onto the dock. They separated as one jumped aboard another silent boat and the other slipped into the cab of a late-model Jeep before it sped away.

"Lauren Cole . . . Miss Lauren Cole . . . please come to a white paging telephone."

Lauren's pulse quickened when she recognized her name. She hooked a thumb under the strap of her soft leather shoulder bag, took a firmer grip on the handle of her cosmetic case, and hurried through the corridor to find a courtesy phone. When she placed the handset to her ear, a buzz sounded; then she heard a click.

"I'm Lauren Cole. I think I heard—"

"Your party is waiting at the Alaskan Airlines ticket counter."

"My bro—" A click on the line ended the conversation before Lauren was through.

"Thanks." She addressed the inanimate handset as though it were a rude stranger, and replaced it on the receiving hook.

Her brother had missed meeting her at the gate. She expected that from Mark. No doubt he had made his way to the ticket counter instead.

People charged past in all directions. Heading toward the ticket area, Lauren merged into the crowd that teemed and surged like rush-hour traffic on San Diego's Mission Bay Highway.

It has to be her. He cocked his head. *She looks like California. But she doesn't look much like Mark—other than those eyes. She certainly dresses the part. California hip.*

For just an instant he was reminded of the day his new bride had arrived. Similarly attired, she had been no more prepared for the shock of their new home than Mark's sister appeared to be. *She* had lasted three weeks. *I wonder how long Mark's sister will last?*

He checked the photograph Mark had lent him. Crinkled and cracked, it was outdated, but her face and smile were unmistakable. He studied her again. There was no mistaking those eyes.

He watched her walk—more like a glide. A tightness grew in his stomach as she neared. She moved low in the hips as she took one smooth step at a time. He gauged her to be shorter than Mark. Five-five, five-seven maybe. With those wedge-heeled sandals, he couldn't be certain. Her hair seemed lighter than her picture showed, and curlier.

The sandals will be the first thing to go. That blouse— his gaze wandered the curves that filled the material in appealing contours—*will be the second. The mosquitoes would eat her alive. Her pants won't do, except in the airport.*

If she's anything like Mark—flamboyant, reckless, always looking for a good time—we are in for a heck of a summer! He shook his head. Mark said she was his little sister. He didn't believe that. She didn't look like anyone's little sister. She'd be a handful. *That* he could believe.

Don't forget that's why you're here, buddy. Get her on the boat as soon as possible and under Mark's wing. She's his problem. Not yours.

As Lauren neared the ticket counter, she again searched the area for her brother, but Mark did not appear among the men who stared back.

Small groups of travelers clustered around the airline booths—most of them dressed in Northwestern apparel of bold plaid shirts, boots, and camping outerwear. The uniformed airline employees seemed curiously out of place to Lauren; she felt equally conspicuous wearing a bright coral-colored knit shirt. In San Diego, her attire assured anonymity; here she stood out like a stray poppy in a field of forest greens.

Unlike Mark, she did not enjoy the feeling of being alone in a strange place, unprepared for what lay ahead. Being vulnerable to the unexpected was not part of the Alaskan experience she wanted.

When she reached the ticket counter, a tall, rugged-looking man caught her attention. Like many locals, he wore faded denims, boots, and a wool shirt. Leaning against the counter, he rested his hands inside the pockets of a bulky vest. Dark hair formed a meticulously groomed beard and mustache on his tanned face. Mirror-lensed sunglasses hid eyes that seemed to be watching her as she approached.

"Darn!" Lauren muttered. "Now what?"

"Looking for someone?" the man behind the sunglasses asked.

"My brother. I was told to meet him here."

A smile spread across the man's face, exposing Tom Selleck teeth and dimples that began at his cheekbones and vanished into his beard. To Lauren, this northerner seemed far too amused by her discomfort.

"Your brother Mark?" he asked, shoving himself away from the counter.

"Yes. Do you know him?"

The stranger removed his sunglasses, slid a large hand from his vest, and offered it. "Name's Buckner. Mark asked me to pick you up."

"Buckner?" His silver-gray eyes glittered. She hesitated, eyeing him dubiously, remembering her brother's favorite baseball team and player. "As in *Bill* Buckner—Kansas City Royals?"

His rich-timbered laugh sent a shiver up her arm as her small hand vanished into the crush of his. "As in Steve. Period!"

"This is a joke, isn't it?" Lauren pivoted, expecting to see Mark rush at her from behind a post. *This is just like him—talk some compliant stranger into playing a trick on me. Very funny!* She wished she had a baseball bat to greet Mark. "Okay, where is he?"

"He's not here."

Buckner reached for her cosmetics case, but Lauren protectively drew it to her side.

"Don't worry. I'm not a kidnapper, thief, or a Kansas City *Royal*. Let me take that for you." He folded his fingers over hers on the handle to take possession of it, his knuck-

les brushing against a gleaming brass plate with the initials
L. C. monogrammed in a flowery script.

"L. C., huh? I used to know a girl with monogrammed
luggage."

"It's a common practice in the civilized world—monograms." Lauren regretted the remark the instant she
watched his smile drop to a frown.

"Yeah, she was the same way. Monograms and designer
clothes." He turned and headed in a direction opposite the
way she had come.

"Listen, I'm—"

"Sorry," he finished. "Me too. Come on; Mark's waiting for us. Let's go."

"My bags . . ."

"Right. We're on our way to baggage; then we'll head
out. We have to hurry."

Although Lauren preferred to carry the case that held the
bulk of her money inside, she didn't think she should risk
insulting him further, so she struggled to stay close behind.
Soon she was hopping to keep up with his long strides,
taking two short steps to each of his as he led her double-
time through the busy International Airport.

Still wishing Mark would show up and end this charade,
Lauren trained her gaze on every man of Mark's height and
build. Her scrutiny met only reciprocal stares and come-on
smiles. Inwardly, she groaned.

Metal-framed posters, the only decorations on otherwise
bare walls, showed women clad in traditional Russian cos-
tumes, and boasted the heritage of "The Last Frontier." It
occurred to Lauren that Buckner had done well to pick her
out among the thousands of faces in the airport.

"How'd you recognize me?"

"You mean before I saw your initials?" Lauren lowered
her eyes as she digested his remark. "Your brother gave a
good description. He said, 'She looks like me except she's

blond and she's a girl. If she looks like she just walked out of San Diego and she's lost, that's her.' ''

Lauren shook her head. *That sounds like Mark, all right.*

''And he gave me this.'' Steve flashed her high school graduation photograph that Mark had obviously kept in his wallet.

''Do you judge everyone on the basis of their luggage?''

''No, I don't. Just some women prefer to carve everything into stone—including their name.''

''Recently divorced?''

''A long time ago.''

Obviously not long enough.

On the plane, Lauren had accepted a California champagne that made her less in control than she liked. The effervescent drink dulled her sensitivity. Now her legs tingled, felt a little weak.

Steve veered to the right, and Lauren found herself face-to-face with a polar bear, its mouth snarling open, massive paws, bigger than her head, suspended to attack. Startled, Lauren screamed.

Steve eyed her silently; then, before she recovered from her shock, he moved on.

''Wait a minute,'' she said, panting. ''I'm not used to this altitude or something. Can you slow down?''

''We're going to be late if we don't move it.''

He maintained his long-legged stride as the pair rushed toward the down escalator. Reaching the ground floor, they rounded a corner and found the airline monitor indicating that her baggage would soon arrive.

Lauren fought to regain her composure while suppressing her need to gasp for air. ''So where is Mark?''

''He had to finish outfitting the boat. I have to get you into Dillingham before the season opens. We don't have much time.''

''Don't they fish all summer?''

"You'll have to catch the tide, or miss the first fishing period."

Lauren's reserved exterior crumbled against the resonance of Steve's deep, masculine voice. It vibrated the air and made her uncomfortably aware of their gender difference. She stole a sidelong glance.

Steve held his head like royalty, aloof and unperturbed by the commotion around him. Dark hair brushed the stiff woolen collar of his shirt and curled slightly above it. She found herself wondering how it would feel to comb her fingers through it. From only a few feet away it looked thick and soft, unlike Richard's short-cropped yuppie look. *Richard!*

He would love to see her flustered, confused, and concerned. He didn't want her to chase after her brother—one more time. But he didn't understand how it was between Lauren and Mark. He didn't understand they were twins. He didn't understand at all.

Lauren shot back to reality at the same time a heavy box hit the side of the luggage carousel with a thud. She recognized her mauve-colored duffel bag as it plummeted down the chute, and pointed at the bag when it landed with an equally loud thud against the stainless-steel circular wall.

"Yours?" Steve asked, returning her case.

She nodded.

He grabbed and swung the heavy bag over the side, dropping it at her feet.

"Whoa. What have you got in here? Rocks? This must weigh a hundred pounds."

Heads turned and Lauren's embarrassment again surfaced. She placed a finger to her lips. "Books," she whispered, hoping to keep the growing audience to a minimum.

Steve caught the attention of a nearby elderly lady and spoke loudly enough for several people to hear. "She likes to read. Her first trip to wild, woolly Alaska, so she thought she had to bring her own library.''

A chorus of chuckles rooted Lauren to the tile beneath her feet. She squeezed her eyes closed to shut out her humiliation.

''Is that it?'' he asked.

''There's one more.'' She frowned. ''Look, I don't want to bother you, buccaneer, and I certainly wouldn't ask you—''

''No bother.'' He scooted the duffel bag closer with the toe of his boot.

''That's mine.'' She reached for the matching canvas suitcase, but Steve grabbed the handle before she could.

''I can get that,'' she told him.

''I'd rather carry that than your cosmetics case,'' he answered. Applying a firm grip to her suitcase, he heaved the duffel bag onto his shoulder and sliced his way through the crowd.

Lauren narrowed her gaze to the broad shoulders and erect head of the tall man in front of her. Like the captain of a ship, he walked as if he knew exactly who he was and never doubted his capabilities. She drew a deep breath and blinked her eyes.

The man transformed into a living, breathing buccaneer. He became a swashbuckling pirate bound for his clipper ship, shouldering his seabag and gear, his swagger appropriate as he navigated in knee-high boots, sword dangling at his side.

She imagined those long arms locked around her, easily lifting her against his salty-smelling ruffled silk shirt— *Wait a minute.* She squelched her daydream and shook her head in disbelief. *What is the matter with me?* The logical side of her brain took over and ousted the dreamy romantic. The vision ended—and Lauren silently vowed *never* to touch champagne again.

Studying the confident man ahead of her, she endured a sudden rush of contradictory feelings.

He's rude.

Considerate.

Conceited.

All male! She argued with herself. He was undeniably attractive with his dark hair and tan. The analytical side of her had the final say. *Hands off!*

Steve stopped beside a waiting taxi. ''Merrill Field,'' he instructed the driver.

The cabbie nodded.

''We're going where?'' Lauren asked.

''Dillingham.''

''By car?''

''Another airport,'' Steve responded, as he opened the door for her.

He placed her bags inside the opened trunk, then joined Lauren in the backseat. The sudden contact of his thigh against hers shot sparks of excitement through Lauren until she discreetly edged her leg away, forcing a space between them.

Lauren smelled spruce. Not a man's cologne, but the pungent, sharp odor of freshly cut wood, and she wondered about Steve's occupation. The aroma, mixed with the strong visual impact of his northern attire, scattered what was left of her weakened defenses in a double-barreled blast.

Lauren tried to concentrate on her surroundings and memorize the route they took from the airport. It seemed as though they traveled in a northeasterly direction, but with the heavy cloud cover she couldn't be sure. They drove through tundra fields; then a beautiful lake appeared on the left side of the road.

''Lake Hood,'' Steve explained.

Shortly, they turned left onto Minnesota Street. Driving

through a cluttered commercial area of one-story weathered stucco buildings, they found themselves penetrating an area of wooden storefronts, brightly lit by flashing neon signs.

After a few minutes of awkward silence, Lauren asked, "What do you do for a living? Did you meet Mark fishing?"

Lauren saw Steve's gaze shift from outside the cab onto her. She could almost feel his touch. Self-consciously, she crossed her arms. Slate gray eyes focused on the solitaire diamond that sparkled from an old-fashioned setting on the ring finger of her left hand.

To Steve, it declared her off-limits. Almost. The high school picture of her that Mark had given him didn't do her justice. She had no business being here, in spite of what Mark explained about her needing a working vacation. He should have suggested something more appropriate, like working as a cruise director on a Caribbean-bound liner. *Man, she's pretty enough. Yeah . . . get a grip, man!*

"He didn't tell you?"

"Tell me what?"

"We're partners. We fish together."

"But . . ." Lauren's brain scrambled to take in this information. "I thought he needed my help. He told me—"

"We usually fish together," Steve corrected. "I've got other things to take care of, and Mark needed help when I wasn't available. I'm surprised he didn't tell you. I sure heard about you."

His voice resounded between them, again stirring a dizzying warmth inside her. His grin widened, and Lauren wondered exactly what it was that Mark would tell a stranger about his only sister. She dreaded the thought. That at twenty-five she led a straight and basically boring routine life? More than likely. Did he mention she was engaged to be married to someone he didn't like? What Mark didn't know was that Richard had canceled their engagement because she had insisted on spending the summer in Alaska. Richard had ordered her not to go. That had done it! She couldn't refuse her twin brother's plea for help. And, now, after all this, she learned she was just a fill-in for a man who obviously didn't want her around.

"Have you ever been fishing?" Steve asked.

"No. I mean . . . not really."

"You've *never* been fishing?"

"Trout," she answered defensively. The look he gave her confirmed that didn't count.

"Ever been on a boat?"

"Sure. Lots of boats."

"Waterskiing? Around San Diego?"

"Point Loma, Mission Bay."

Lauren shifted uneasily in her seat, wishing she were out of this seedy, used sedan and headed back home.

"And you're here because . . . ?"

"Mark asked me to—"

"Right."

"It can't be that hard to fish, can it?" Lauren persisted. "I mean, Mark seemed to think—"

"Unfortunately, too many people come here looking for big money, but don't realize it takes lots of hard work."

"I know how to work." Lauren's throat tightened. The long trip, Steve's tone of voice, and the champagne all combined to work against her.

"All I know is that Mark asked me to pick you up and deliver you to Dillingham. What happens after that is between the two of you. Unless it affects *my* business," he added.

So that's it! Lauren turned her head to the window and fumed. *How could Mark think of asking me to join him without clearing it with his partner? Unless Mark wanted to keep it from him. Mark said something about having problems, but what did he mean? Trouble with his partner?*

Lauren considered flying back to Richard and San Diego where she belonged, but knew she wouldn't. Mark wouldn't have called for help if he hadn't needed her. There must be more to this fishing venture than either her brother or Buckner was telling her, and Lauren wasn't comfortable with any part of it.

When they reached the municipal airport, Steve unloaded her bags and paid the fare; then the cab sped away, leaving its passengers alone in front of a misty airfield.

Lauren followed Steve to a shiny low-wing Mooney trimmed in red and orange parked by an open hangar. He climbed onto a wing and wrestled Lauren's heavy baggage into an empty space behind the seats.

"Need help getting in?"

Lauren eyed the small seat suspiciously. When she didn't answer, he walked away, leaving her to seat herself. Lauren hoisted herself onto the wing step and climbed into the cockpit. She caught a glimpse of Steve as he disappeared inside the hangar office. He soon reemerged with a slightly built man who wore mechanic's overalls. As they drew closer, Lauren mentally compared the two. Steve's six-foot-plus frame dwarfed the other man, even though he also looked tall.

"Duke, this is Mark's sister, Lauren," Steve said. "Lauren, Duke Reilly."

"Pleased to meet you." Duke smiled.

"Likewise." Duke looked like someone Mark would team up with. Face and clothes smeared with grease, baseball cap worn backward on his matted red hair, he showed the same zest and inborn drive Mark had that spelled fun with a capital *F*.

"Are you our pilot?" Lauren asked.

"Nah, I'm a mechanic. I stay on this side of those mountains. They're like women, beautiful but treacher— Uh, sorry, miss. I didn't mean anything by that."

Lauren glanced at Steve as he attempted to conceal a laugh.

"That brother of yours is quite a character—uh, good man. Yeah. I introduced him to ol' Buckner here."

Lauren sensed that Reilly was not comfortable in her presence, but she knew he wasn't trying to be rude as he struggled to censor his remarks.

"I'll let him know I met you," she replied.

"Good. Good." Nervously, he turned to Steve. "It looked like someone had their hands in there, all right, but nothing serious. I tightened a few nuts. I couldn't find anything else wrong. But I'd keep a close eye on it, just the same."

"Will do. Thanks, Duke."

The two men shook hands; then Steve climbed in, fastened his seat belt, and began his preflight check.

Duke leaned toward Lauren's window. "Tell Mark when he's through playing Popeye he's got a job with me. It's a lot safer here than—" He stopped and kicked at an invisible pebble. "Tell him I said hi." Duke waved, then plowed his hands into his pockets, sauntering back toward his office.

"What'd he mean by that?"

"Duke's a flatlander. He doesn't trust mountains, boats, or women. Buckle up."

Lauren fastened her seat belt and settled in for takeoff.

"Where'd you learn to fly? Were you—"

"Escondido. Cal-West Airlines."

"You weren't in the service?"

"No."

Steve taxied the craft toward the runway, while Lauren surveyed the airfield. Hundreds of planes, anchored securely by thick ropes to metal rings in the ground, lined the parking area. Abruptly, her hands moistened, and she realized she had been gripping the sides of her upholstered bucket seat.

"Scared?"

Lauren felt nervous but shook her head. Duke's comments concerned her, but she resigned herself to simply relaying them to Mark. "I've never flown in a small plane before."

"You'll get used to it. There aren't too many roads outside of town, so we get around by plane. These small planes are safer than jumbo jets. A lot more places to land if you're forced down."

"That's reassuring." *If that's his way of making me relax, I'm in big trouble.*

The engines whined when Steve stopped and waited for clearance. When he received the go-ahead, he guided the plane onto the main runway. Lauren braced herself. The force of acceleration as they surged skyward pressed her back into the seat. Power transmitted from the engines, flowed through her, then seemed to diminish when the wheels left the ground.

"We'll be in the air about two and a half hours. I'll point out some of the landmarks we'll fly over," Steve shouted over the engine noise.

She opened her eyes and saw the anxious look on her face in his mirrored lenses. "Thanks," Lauren shouted back.

Climbing now, they flew over a large body of water, and Steve pointed out Kamishak Bay running into the Gulf of Alaska. Soon, they turned from the Kenai Peninsula and headed southwest toward Dillingham.

After a few minutes in the air, the engines quieted to a drone. "Mark tells me you're a CPA," he said.

"Just passed the exam."

"Oh, yeah?"

"Yes. I'm going to start my own business."

"Up here?"

"No. La Jolla."

Steve nodded. "When?"

"The end of the summer. I leased an office to open September first."

"What are you doing here?"

"I told you, I came to help Mark. He called me."

Steve frowned.

She unconsciously twisted the heirloom on her finger. She and Richard had set their wedding date for Labor Day, but now it was off indefinitely. She was glad she had refused to let Richard buy a ring for her. Her grandmother's ring was the only diamond she ever expected to wear.

They rode in silence for a few minutes before Lauren spoke again. "Are you from around here?"

"California."

She waited for him to resume, but when he didn't, she asked, "How long have you lived in Dillingham?"

"Dad moved up twenty years ago, when he retired. We built a cabin together on the shore of Second Lake outside Aleknagik."

"You live there with your dad?"

"Used to. He's gone now."

A few minutes later, Steve continued, "I used to visit every summer. I liked it so well I decided to stay.

"It's a lot different from San Diego . . . about twelve hundred people. But in the summer the population usually doubles. Fishing season brings at least twelve hundred more from the neighboring villages and the outside. Bristol Bay's gold rush—compliments of the salmon," he added.

Lauren had been traveling since 5:00 A.M. The long trip, the steady hum of the engine, and the lack of rest combined to relax her guard. Her eyelids drooped, and she quickly fell asleep. She had no idea how long she dozed before a high-pitched warning buzzer jarred her awake.

The left engine sputtered. Lauren watched Steve's face for any sign of panic. He appeared calm.

"What's the matter?" Lauren yelled.

Steve rotated a lever on the floor. "Left-tank fuel starvation. I have to switch to the right tank."

Steve stared at the altimeter, then switched his cross-check to the gas gauges in front of him. "Starboard tank's half full. We'll be all right."

Just then a cold wind thermal seized and shuddered the plane. They dropped a few hundred feet before Steve leveled it. Lauren's stomach hung, suspended in midair. She was glad she had not eaten recently, thinking she would have lost it if she had. The engine sputtered again, then caught. Steve brought them to an altitude of 10,000 feet before again leveling the craft.

"You're not trying to scare me, are you?" Lauren demanded. "Part of your initiation ceremony?"

"I wouldn't do that. Whatever clogged the line must've passed with that jolt." Steve smiled. "No big deal."

Steve appeared a more serious type than Mark. That was evident. He took everything on, that she had seen so far, with the cunning and calculation he apparently learned in his former career. She wondered how he and Mark fared as partners. Maybe it wasn't working out. She would find out soon enough.

They flew through a narrow pass in the mountains, skirting sheer cliffs of snow and ice-covered slate. Steve lowered their altitude gradually to 1,400 feet until they seemed to skim barely above the icy flow, like a seagull diving along the beach.

Lauren tensed. "Is the plane all right?"

"Sure. I just thought you'd like a closer look, that's all."

"I can see just fine," Lauren assured him. "Where are we?"

"Lake Clark Pass. It stays frozen all year."

"It's beautiful." Turquoise blue veins of color lined the jagged glacier beneath them. The plane appeared to assume the grace of a bird, effortlessly riding the crests of air between the fierce-looking mountains that bordered them on both sides. Nevertheless, Lauren felt awed by the spectacular scenery.

Steve again focused his attention on the cockpit dials.

"We're about sixty minutes out. Just in time to get you on the boat. Did you bring rain gear?"

Lauren answered him with a blank look.

"Boots?"

She felt as if she'd been caught without her milk money in kindergarten.

"Slicker?"

Lauren swallowed and once more shook her head. Steve looked irritated.

"I'll make sure they're on board before you go." He looked her over. "Size eight shoes?"

Lauren nodded.

"We have twenty-five-foot tidal shifts—did Mark tell you that?"

Lauren's stomach knotted. "No. He didn't."

"Didn't he tell you it's dangerous out there? You could be killed. This is not sunny Cal." His voice rose with his ire. "Last weekend two brothers drowned in Bristol Bay. California boys. Your age. It happens," he stated with finality.

Lauren squirmed and moved closer to the door, trying to force distance between them.

"Those boys got caught in a tidal shift and landed on a sandbar. Their boat literally smashed to pieces when the tide came in. It's no place for beginners."

What have I gotten myself into? I hope Mark knows what he's doing. She glanced at the stone-faced pilot, dreading a sarcastic comment, but Steve remained silent. Minutes passed before he spoke again, his finger pointing north.

"There it is . . . Dillingham."

Lauren stared at the large cliff bordering the south end of the town.

"Down there." He pointed again. "See the cannery?"

A massive metal structure emerged that resembled an old factory. Bloodlike rust stains streaked the sagging metal roof, and a large black wooden dock separated the building from the water.

"We generally take our salmon there, or to Ekuk or Naknek. Depends on where Mark decides to fish. Most of us fish the Naknek area, though. And there's the thriving metropolis."

Lauren's impression of the scene below spawned an old-world feeling of quaintness, purity, and fantasy, as though she had just broken a time barrier and entered the world of fifty years ago.

Steve spoke into his headset microphone and requested permission to land.

"Dead ahead—Dillingham International." He veered the plane toward the dirt runway. The plane's wings remained level when the small tires screeched in unison.

Although her heart beat rapidly in response to her fear, Lauren had to admire the skill and control with which Steve handled his plane. She only wished she felt a micromeasure of confidence for dealing with what lay ahead.

Chapter Two

Lauren maneuvered herself to the opening. The seating space had given no room for movement during the flight, and she was not sure her legs would hold her. She teetered for a moment, then thrust her leg backward out the door, testing the air behind her for the wing step.

A man's powerful hands slipped around her waist from behind. "C'mon down. A little more to the right." She stiffened slightly, missed the step, slid down Steve's long length, and ended up in an unladylike position. For an instant Lauren leaned against him, disoriented, before she disentangled herself to establish her footing. Steve's throaty chuckle embarrassed Lauren. When he let her go, she pitched sideways and accidentally stepped on his foot.

"I'm sorry, Steve, I—"

He steadied her again. She gasped as he pulled her toward him, then desperately searched for a reason to break his hold.

"I'm not."

A wide smile spread slowly across his tanned features. He leaned toward her, and she could again smell the spruce scent on his clothing, feel the heat that permeated his shirt.

Lauren believed he was going to kiss her, when he suddenly turned her around and swatted her behind.

"On your way, kid. Mark's waiting."

"Whoooeee! Lauren! Hey, Lauren!"

Mark whistled and whooped like a mountain man as he jogged across a muddied field waving a gaudy red cap. When he reached his sister, he swung her off her feet and into the air as if they'd rehearsed a fifties dance routine. Lauren hadn't yet adjusted to the landing, and although she had hoped the champagne was wearing off, she rocked precariously when Mark released her.

Steve grinned and slapped Mark on the back. "Here she is. Safe and sound."

"Thanks, guy. What do I owe you?" He fished his wallet from the baggy back pocket of his striped overalls and leafed through a wad of moist green bills.

"A ton of fish. Help me unload her stuff, will you?"

Lauren reached for her bag, but Mark held her back. "Step aside, Lauren. I'll get this."

"We should have rented a front-end loader for the gear she brought along. I never will understand why a woman packs like she's leaving home forever when she goes anywhere."

"Thanks for the ride, Steve. I intend to pay you for your trouble."

He grinned. "Later."

"There you are, Steven," a woman's sultry voice interrupted. She drew the men's attention from Lauren to herself as she circled her arm into Steve's. Although she wore corduroys and a long-sleeved knit shirt, a svelte figure was evident beneath her clothes. Lauren noticed the woman's scarlet-tipped fingers—expertly done, but fake. Looking down at her own buffed but not polished, sensibly cut nails, Lauren self-consciously balled her hands into fists.

It was obvious by the liberty the woman took with Steve that she considered him her private property. Even though they were hidden behind oversize sunglasses, the woman's eyes, Lauren was sure, were as hard as the soles of her expensive leather boots.

Mark said, "Sherry, this is my sister—"

"I know," she said coolly. "I've got the Jeep, Steve. Want a ride into town?"

Steve seemed totally engrossed by the redheaded arm bracelet who had attached herself to him. She had already proven to be rude, catty, and—if Steve's reaction were a standard of measure—bewitching.

"Yeah, sure. You'd better get going, Mark. Those salmon are waiting."

Mark laughed. "And about a hundred other fishermen."

"Just let 'em get a look at your new partner. That'll throw 'em off the track. By the way—did you get extra rain gear on board?"

"No, but I will."

"See you later, L. C.," Steve called as they walked away.

Bristling, Lauren hoisted the large canvas suitcase from the ground and stormed after her brother toward his battered Jeep. She could hear the pair laughing in the distance. When she reached his Jeep, she swung the heavy bag over the side, where it collided against the seats with a ponderous *whump*.

Lauren glanced at Steve, and saw him climb into the passenger's side of a late-model Jeep. Sherry planted a kiss on his mouth, then flipped her flaming red hair back and placed manicured hands on the wheel. Lauren's stomach twisted, and she felt heat rush to her face.

"I thought he wasn't married," she said to Mark when he plopped into the seat beside her.

"He's not."

"Who's she?"

"Sherry Mallory. His bookkeeper. She's real sharp," Mark added, grinning.

"I'll bet." Lauren dismissed the pair. How could Steve hold her the way he had, making Lauren feel so wanted and vulnerable, then walk right into the arms of another woman? Lauren couldn't understand it. In spite of her brother's good humor, Lauren's mood grew as dismal as the overcast sky. Low clouds hovered, not seeming to move, but threatening to spill their load without warning.

Mark steered them onto a well-used dirt-and-gravel road. It was the only road into town, he informed her. He jerked the steering wheel back and forth, dodging potholes, causing Lauren to slide from one side of the slick vinyl bench to the other, as if on a crazy carnival ride.

According to a small green-and-white road sign, Dillingham lay four miles from the airport. Tundra meadows and tall spruce that grew on both sides of the road whizzed by while she clutched the back of her seat.

"Road's a little rough right now. It's been too wet for grading, and before that, the ground was frozen. How was your flight? How are you, anyway?"

Mark rattled his questions off in his typical barrage, as if his mouth struggled to keep up with his brain.

"Buckner was very entertaining. He told me about the tides, the accident last week, asked if I'd brought the proper clothing . . . things like that."

It had been a long year since Lauren had seen Mark. Collar-length brown hair and a newly acquired mustache made her twin appear older than his twenty-five years, but his zest for life made him seem perpetually young.

Mark grinned sheepishly. "Forgot to mention a few things."

"Forgot?"

"Didn't want to scare you," he admitted. "I didn't think you'd come."

"You should have told me everything, Mark. Now I am scared, and it's too late to do anything about it."

"I wanted you to come. If I'd told you everything, you wouldn't have."

"You're right, I wouldn't have."

"So I'm forgiven?"

"Come clean with me," Lauren demanded.

"OK." He patted her hand. "There's something fishy going on."

Lauren raised a brow and she laughed in spite of the seriousness of their discussion. "Come on, Mark. I could do better than that."

"Well, I mean fishier than usual."

"You told me there was some kind of trouble. What is it?"

Mark became unusually reflective.

"Does it have something to do with the brothers who died last week?"

"I needed you to help me fish. I thought you probably needed a vacation from what's-his-name."

"Richard."

"Yeah, and that firm you're working for."

"Buckner says you needed a replacement for when he's not fishing with you. I didn't know anything about that. And," she added, "you failed to mention that he was your partner. How do you think I felt when I found out I was stepping into his territory?"

"I didn't think about that. I just knew you had to be here."

"Mark." Lauren struggled for patience. "What exactly is the problem?"

"I think someone is juggling the books. I think there's sabotage in the fleet, and I think that you can help me figure it out. It could be my imagination, but there are just too many coincidences, and you know me. I'll take all the chances in the world, but I just have a feeling . . .''

"What about Buckner? Do you trust him?"

"He's my partner. If I lose, he loses."

"Who owns the boat?" Lauren asked.

"We both do. Fifty-fifty."

"You both make payments?"

"I make them to him; he owns the title."

"And his bookkeeper, Sherry . . . Mim—Mam—Mal—"

"Mallory. She and her dad have been in the area for years. I don't think they're a problem."

"Anybody else you know or don't know?"

"Not that I've met."

"Mark, get serious. We're talking murder here."

"I know." A frown crossed Mark's face. "I don't know what to think. I'm not sure it was a good idea to bring you here after all."

"This isn't going to turn out to be some very expensive joke on your sister, is it?"

He answered her with a don't-you-trust-me look. Mark shifted his gaze forward, then said, "Tell you what—we don't have time now, but I'll sneak you into the office when we get back."

"Sneak?" Lauren wailed. "Mark, if Steve is honest, why don't you just ask him for an accounting? If you don't have a good relationship, perhaps you should retain a lawyer."

"I'd rather you just check it out on the side. If there are discrepancies, you'll find them. I don't want to ruin a good thing with Steve if I'm wrong."

Lauren eyed his faded T-shirt, once navy blue. He wore a blue-and-white bandanna knotted around his throat. With a red mechanic's rag stuffed halfway into his overalls pocket, he reminded Lauren of a rodeo clown. All he lacked was the painted face. She couldn't stay at odds with him. They were twins, after all.

"You'll help me, won't you?" Mark asked.

"I'll do what I can. But this sounds serious. You may want the police involved."

"Promise you'll check it out first. If we're over our heads, then we'll call the cops."

"Dillingham has a police force, hasn't it?"

"Basically."

"All right. I'll do what I can, but promise you'll follow through."

"You know I will."

"Uncross your fingers."

Mark laughed.

"It's good to see you, Mark." Lauren hugged him around his seat-belted waist, then moved back to her side of the seat. "You might have told me about Buckner, though. He really didn't seem pleased about your choice of fishing partners."

"You don't take up much room."

"He's not fishing with us?"

"You don't like that idea? Oh, yeah, what's-his-name might not approve, huh?" Mark looked at her, eyes twinkling. "Let's not tell him, okay?"

"Really, Mark."

"We'll have a good time, and then you can go back to who's-it. . . ."

"Richard."

Mark paused for half a heartbeat.

"Did Steve meet you at the gate?"

"Ticket counter. I met Duke Reilly too, said he was a friend of yours."

"So, what d'ya think of Steve?"

"Arrogant, rude, and, if you want my opinion—"

''Look, Lauren. There's a fox.''

Lauren looked but didn't see anything.

''Arctic fox. Keep your eyes peeled. We might see another. Have to be fast, though.''

''As I was saying—''

''Aw, don't take Steve too seriously, Lauren. I'm sure he didn't mean anything personal.

He probably had his mind on something else. He was happy to pick you up. I've talked about you enough.''

''Did you tell him I was engaged to Richard?''

''How is he anyway?''

Lauren wasn't sure if or how she was going to tell Mark about Richard and his ultimatum. She had toyed with the idea, but didn't believe it would serve any useful purpose for Mark to know he had come between her and her fiancé.

''He thinks you're going to change my mind about marrying him.''

''He knows me too well. I'll have to change my tack.''

Lauren changed the subject. ''How about you, Mark? When are you going to settle down?''

''Why should I? After you get rich working up here, you can start your own business and support me when I get old and gray.''

''You're not the grasshopper—I'm not the ant,'' Lauren chided.

''Yeah, but you're my only family, and you're gorgeous, and I'm so glad to see you.''

Mark's flattery ended what could've turned into a serious conversation. He avoided seriousness with the same skill he applied to getting out of dishwashing and nine-to-five jobs. Lauren decided to let it drop. ''So when do we leave?''

''King salmon season started May twenty-fifth, but we should be able to get in on some of it yet. It lasts till the middle of June, generally, and if we're lucky, till the middle of July. We go back out the last of June for the red salmon—that's the main run, and that goes till the second week in July. This year the chum are running too, so we'll have a full season. They only run once every four years.''

Lauren only half listened. She didn't even know what a salmon looked like—just that it was bigger than a trout.

''The humpies,'' Mark continued, ''are the pink salmon. They run the first week of August, so between periods of open and closed seasons you'll be busy.''

''*We'll* be busy, you mean.''

''Right. We have a lot of work ahead of us. We'll be through probably by August twenty-fifth; then I'll take a few days and get *Ivy* ready for dry storage.''

''Good. That'll give me a few days to get my lease settled and—''

''If you go back to San Diego,'' Mark corrected her. ''I told you we'd make so much money we can retire . . . till next year, that is.''

Lauren laughed at her brother's plan. ''Really, Mark. I'm starting a business. On schedule. I told you that.''

''You don't believe me, do you?'' He sounded offended.

''That I won't have to go back to work? Let's just say it would be nice, but I'm not going to plan on it until it actually happens.''

''Listen, if we do well, we can easily clear a few thousand each.''

''You've come up with more get-rich-quick ideas than anybody I've ever met. If I make enough this summer to pay for my trip home, I'll be eternally grateful,'' she said, giving him a playful nudge. ''I'm not counting on becoming independently wealthy over this.''

Mark laughed and howled like a coyote. ''Welcome aboard, mate.''

Bouncing along toward the fishing community in the dark green vintage Jeep, Lauren let her mind fill with thoughts of Steve Buckner, while Mark rattled nonstop about the fishing, the local hotel, the people she would meet, and the good times they would have when the season was over. She caught only bits of his conversation, and, before long, they had arrived.

The road widened into a *V* bordered on both sides by full running streams of rainwater. Brown pools of muddied water dotted the road, indicating large potholes that Mark dodged.

A vehicle traveling west out of town bounced into one and sloshed dirty water on the Jeep as they passed. A second car, an early-model American sedan, honked, and the driver waved at Mark before her brother wheeled in front of one of the two hotels in town.

The hand brake squawked when Mark pulled it back; then he cut the engine. ''Emily runs the Briarwood.''

Lauren's eyebrows shot upward in response to the ancient-looking two-story hotel. A large wooden sign worn by weather and wind bore faded blue letters on a peeling white background that heralded *Briarwood Hotel.*

Chunks of brown-painted stucco had broken from the building, exposing weatherworn wood framing. Weeds grew around the base of the hotel, taking on the appearance of flowered landscaping. A large brown puddle that surrounded the cement porch made a clean entrance to the hotel impossible. She had avoided buildings like this in California, afraid of the derelicts that lived inside.

''Mark, this is terrible. Are you sure it's safe?''

Mark laughed. ''You're going to do a lot of things you never thought possible before this summer ends. I'd take you around town, but we really don't have time. We have to pull out before the tide shifts.''

A plump, gray-haired woman met the twins at the doorway. ''Emmie, this is my sister, Lauren.'' Dressed in a pastel cotton house shift and stained apron, the woman hugged them both.

"Welcome to Dillingham, dear. Mark told me you were coming to help him fish. You must be tired from the long trip." Emily produced a small potpie from behind the counter. "The diner is already closed, and I thought you might be hungry, so I baked this for you."

Surprised, Lauren accepted the food. "Thank you. That was very nice of you."

"Well, I've been looking forward to meeting you, dear. Mark thinks the world of you."

"Thanks for the grub, Emmie," Mark said. "I was in such a hurry I didn't think about that."

"I don't suppose I'll be seeing you two for a while." Emily chuckled. "Take good care of her, Mark. Good luck fishing, you two."

Mark nodded. "I'll leave the key up front after we're out, Emily." Mark led the way down a long, dark hall and fitted a brass key into the old doorknob lock. "The tide will be in about thirty minutes from now. You should change and I'll be back in a few."

"Where are you going?" Lauren asked.

"I won't be long."

Mark set her duffel bag on top of the small twin bed and left the room.

As she unzipped her bag, he stuck his head back into the room and said, "You may want to take a shower, because we don't have one on board. Bathroom's down the hall, but make it quick. We'll leave as soon as you're ready." Mark shut the door behind him and left her alone in the small room.

"Down the hall?" Lauren took another look around the hotel room. There was no bathroom.

Boy, oh, boy. She shook her head. *Things get worse by the minute.*

Peering out from her doorway, Lauren checked to see if anyone was there. Beige-flecked tile shone between muddied footprints the full length of the fifty-foot hallway. With the other doors closed, the hotel seemed cold, harsh, and deserted. Had it not been for Emily's warm welcome, Lauren would have felt completely abandoned. She ducked back inside her room.

The delicious smell of the potpie diverted Lauren's attention to her growling stomach; Emily had provided a fork and a napkin, so she set upon her dinner. After she had eaten, Lauren gathered a change of clothes from her duffel bag. Some of the books she'd brought along had to be removed to allow Lauren access to a long-sleeved turtleneck that she would wear. As she balanced a thick volume in her hand, Steven's presence invaded the room in a replay of his words in the International Airport. *Her first trip to wild, woolly Alaska, so she thought she had to bring her own library.* Lauren slammed the book on the bed.

A freestanding white porcelain sink and bevel-edged mirror afforded some individual privacy, but Lauren decided she would shower. A chrome wire rack displayed an assortment of clean, white, but very thin towels. She chose a towel and washcloth, then studied herself in the mirror. Her face reflected the tiredness she felt, by the deepened furrow between her brows that seemed exaggerated when she was tired, worried, or, like now, feeling out of her element. It had been there as long as she could remember, even in her baby pictures. It was indelibly etched onto her face as though she were trying to view the world from too serious a perspective, while she remembered her twin's smiling face beside her, his eyes squeezed shut by his ear-to-ear smile.

She picked at the curls that framed her soft features, then straightened the collar on her blouse. Just for a moment, Lauren allowed herself the luxury of feeling sorry for herself. She had virtually thrown away her chance to marry a secure, stable, reasonably attractive corporate attorney. For what? A trip to Alaska because her brother called and said he needed her?

But, the voice inside her head argued, *if Richard really loved you he wouldn't have ordered you not to go. He wouldn't have canceled the engagement.*

Lauren sighed, tired of it all. She had spent hours analyzing his conditions and her responses, and it had gotten her nowhere. She pushed her concerns aside one more time and busied herself with the matter at hand. She had a boat to catch.

Lauren wandered down the hall until she found a large *Bathroom* sign on the door. It was clean, albeit old. The fixtures appeared to be fifties vintage, but there was good water pressure, and she enjoyed a quick, hot shower.

She quickly changed her clothes, rearranged her belongings, and rushed to meet Mark in the lobby. She heard the squawk of his hand brake and saw him leaping over the side of his doorless Jeep about the same time she entered the room.

''Ready, Lauren?''

''As ready as I'll ever be. I got all my things.''

''I picked up an extra slicker for you, and boots.''

''Good.''

''Let's go.''

Mark kicked up gravel and dirt when he sped away from the Briarwood. They headed through the middle of town, then veered south and entered a fenced parking area.

''We'll leave the Jeep here while we're out. I paid for my space ahead of time,'' Mark explained.

Mark helped Lauren carry her bags as they waded through a marshy area that opened up toward the dock. At least twenty boats bobbed and strained against their lines as the tide rose in the bay. Mark leaped over the bottom step and landed on the dock, even though the bags he shouldered were uneven weights.

"There's the *Ivy*," he called behind him. "See it?"

Murky, gray-green waves slapped against the mooring dock where the *Ivy* waited, anchored. A new white paint job trimmed in a bright green-and-gold ivy motif distinguished Mark's boat from the others in the harbor.

"What a cute little boat."

Mark disappeared onto the deck and below into the crew quarters, then reappeared.

"Like it?"

"This looks like your work, Mark. Did you do the trim?"

"Sure did. You should have seen it before. It was a mess. But I'm proud of this little boat. We've gotten to be good friends." Mark fingered the manual throttle on the large diesel engine, revving it to borderline rpms. He emerged from the engine compartment, his smile lighting his face like sunshine breaking through Alaska's constant clouds.

"There. I just finished adjusting the idle. Everything else is set. I had the radio worked on. Got it back yesterday, so we're ready to go."

Lauren was excited to see Mark engaged so completely in his work. He had worked as a mechanic in California, but the everyday routine, constant moderate temperatures, and lack of challenge had driven him to search for a more exciting life. It seemed he had found it. She felt slightly envious.

"This works for you, doesn't it, Mark?"

"The boat? Of course."

"Your life here. You seem so happy."

"Having you here completes the picture, Lauren. I didn't realize how much I missed having you around."

"I would've thought you'd be tired of me, holding you

back, worrying about your shenanigans, trying to keep us both out of trouble.''

Mark laughed. ''You're my favorite sister. How could I ever get tired of you?''

Lauren shook her head. Even though their personalities were vastly different, there was always going to be that inexplicable bond they shared as twins that made them tolerant of each other's differences.

''There are two canvas coats in the shelf above your bunk. Get them for us and make sure all your gear is secured. There may be rough water ahead—you don't want your things scattered all over the cabin.''

Lauren ducked below and searched their quarters. Two bunks lined each wall, allowing sleeping quarters for four people. She found the raingear, coats, and hats, then made a quick check of the area. The stove burners and cabinet doors were locked in place, but her red down jacket lay on top of her bunk, so she tucked it underneath the heavy Army surplus bag that was already in the cabin.

The dark cabin smelled of mildew. Understandably, Lauren thought. Always subject to moisture-laden air, it reeked of the musty odor. Lauren preferred the fresh air on deck to that in the cramped quarters. Still weary from the long flight, she seemed to be operating on her second wind, helped by the wholesome dinner Emily had provided. When she was finally able to sleep, Lauren thought, she would sleep hard—smell or no smell.

''All secured, Mark.''

Her brother had already taken his position at the round captain's wheel beneath the colorful green cab. ''All right. Take your position on deck,'' he ordered. ''We're off.''

Lauren was too engrossed with their cruise through Dillingham's harbor, the exhilaration of wind blowing across the boat, and her brother's nonchalant handling of the thirty-two-foot fishing vessel, to think about Steve or

Richard or any other problems. All too soon they left the comparatively quiet water of the cove, and charged head-first through what appeared to be nine- to ten-foot waves. The *Ivy*'s narrow bow lifted at a sharp forty-five-degree angle as it broke through the dark water. Down they rode into a trough, then up again to crash through yet another wall of water.

After about half an hour, the jolting, merciless ride assaulted Lauren's stomach. Hammering waves brought on a nauseous feeling that threatened to overcome her. Her legs ached trying to maintain her balance. Muscles quivered with the unusual strain, like the times when she had pushed herself too long for the day when waterskiing. She had to sit down.

Mark peered over his shoulder at his sister, then back at the dangerous waves in front of him. "You'd better get below. You look a little green."

"You think I'm seasick?" It didn't seem possible to her. She had sailed in the Pacific around San Diego several times, but had never experienced this. "Is this normal? Is it always this rough out here?" Lauren fought to control her nausea. The breakers pounding against the boat seemed to roar.

"This isn't bad. The tide's just starting to change. Better get below before you fall."

Lauren hesitated, not wanting to confine herself in the cramped, moldy smelling cabin. She stayed outside as long as she could. Her head swam dizzily, and she clung stiff-armed to the side of the sturdy little boat. Lauren felt the color drain from her face; then a warm rush of heat flooded her cheeks.

"Mark . . . I think I—" Motion sickness overwhelmed her, and Lauren leaned over the rail to lose her dinner. A second wave of nausea hit her as the boat crashed into another swell.

"Are you all right?" Mark called behind him. "I can't leave the wheel, Lauren."

"Yeah," she struggled to say. She retched again, but it seemed to relieve the queasiness. Wiping the rough canvas raincoat sleeve across her face, she nodded her head weakly. "I'm all right. I think I'll lie down . . . I've never been seasick before."

Lauren felt devastated. She had proven herself an unworthy seaman, and they hadn't even been in the water an hour. "I won't be sick the whole time, will I?"

"Nah. That happened to me the first time I went out. Don't feel bad. You'll get over it. Go on down and rest. I don't need you topside right now."

Lauren nodded and swung her head under the low-beamed doorway. She lay down on her bunk and drew her knees to her chest. When at last they reached the smooth waters of Nushagak Inlet, Lauren was able to relax fully. The unnerving queasiness subsided and exhaustion took its place. As she anticipated, sleep encompassed her like wrappings on a newborn; she slept, oblivious to everything around her.

Despite the fact that it was early June, the evening temperature was cool, and the skies were cloudy, unlike San Diego. The surplus military bag lay heavily on her, but she was glad for the comforting weight, assured it wouldn't slip off during the night. Mark anchored their boat and waited with the multitude of fishermen for the regulated time of open season.

Chapter Three

Lauren molded herself to the well-dressed man in her dreams. Overtaken by her nearness, Richard kissed her sweetly. When she lifted her face her eyes merged with the gray-eyed man who now wore Alaskan plaid. White teeth flashed in a captivating smile. Buckner! His image disappeared when she was jolted awake by what sounded like a booming crash against the side of the boat, followed by a volley of shouting, and deep-throated boat horns.

Her heart pounding like a steam engine, Lauren scrubbed dew from her tiny, circular porthole to peer outside. Through the mist, she saw people waving flashlights, then heard yelling as their boats rushed past the *Ivy.*

Fear immobilized her as she tried to shake the filmy scene from her eyes and make sense of what she saw. *They're really close,* she thought. *Too close.* Another boat careened toward them dangerously, missing them by inches.

"Mark! Hey, Mark . . ." Lauren leaped from her bed and shook her brother. "Wake up! Those people are crazy out there. They're trying to hit us!"

Lauren screamed and struggled to maintain her balance,

rousing Mark from sleep as their boat crashed with a wrenching thud against the side of another boat.

''What the—'' Mark threw off his sleeping bag and charged up the stairs to the main deck.

''What are they doing?'' Lauren shouted.

''Oh, no!''

Lauren heard Mark sprint to the stern, then back to the helm.

''The anchor's loose. Get up here and help me steer.''

Mark started the engine and held it on full throttle until Lauren could relieve him.

Lauren's heart pounded hard. It was cold, dark, and damp outside. She had slept fully clothed, except for her shoes, and the moisture on the deck saturated her socks before she'd gone ten feet. She took the helm from Mark. Huddling close to the wheel, she held the throttle wide-open against the fast-flowing tide, trying to hold their position and avoid the other boats in the channel.

Mark wrenched the anchor line hand over hand, quickly hauling it aboard. It seemed he managed several tasks in one motion, and she saw a flash of iron as he heaved the heavy anchor over the bow and into the fast-moving water. The boat jerked to a halt when the anchor caught. Following Mark's orders, Lauren eased the throttle back. The anchor seemed to hold.

Mark returned to the cab and relieved Lauren of the wheel.

''Man! I thought I had that secured. It must have come loose.''

''I thought you did too,'' she said, looking around them. All the other boats seemed unaffected by the tide that flowed into the bay.

''It happens occasionally,'' he explained. ''That's one of the hazards of mooring in the river with such a big tide. It's not that uncommon.''

"I thought they were crashing into us!" Lauren's voice quaked. The hammering of her heart receded as she realized that they were now safe.

"I'm glad we were so far up the inlet. If we hadn't hit those boats, we could've drifted into the fishing area. Fish and Game could've picked us up for trespassing."

"You mean—"

"If we're caught in the area out of the specific time period, we're in trouble. That would've knocked us out for the season," Mark said, shaken. "C'mon. Let's get some sleep. Season opens at three-thirty."

Lauren groaned. The last twenty-four hours had taken her from her sunny apartment in San Diego, to rocking on a fishing boat in semidark, cold, predawn Alaska. *Time is moving too fast for me,* she decided as she stumbled back to her bunk. She changed her socks, slipped her down jacket on, and crawled into the warm bag, drawing her knees to her chest in an attempt to warm herself.

Sleep, she thought tiredly. *Let me sleep.* Her thoughts once again homed in on the dark-haired man. *He's dangerous,* the voice inside her head prattled. *He wants Sherry,* it taunted. *He'll break your heart,* it warned.

Lauren wriggled deeper inside her sleeping bag, noisily obstructing the troublesome chattering in her head. "Good night again, Mark. See you in the morning." She drew the bag over her head and willed herself to sleep.

She didn't remember hearing Mark's answer before she succumbed to the dreamless world that enveloped her. Two short hours later, Mark shook his sister.

"Get up, Lauren. We've got to move it." He dashed upstairs to start the engine. "Get some coffee going, will you?"

"Yeah. Okay." The last thing she remembered was shivering before she fell asleep thinking about her soft, warm bed in San Diego. *I could be sipping orange juice on my patio, or taking a long hot shower if I were home,* she mused.

Richard usually called her about this time and they'd make plans for lunch. She knew how he operated. On schedule: his coffee, prepared the night before, set to perk at the same time each day. Wing-tip shoes, tie, and designer shirts were his style. His clothing, like his career, spoke of success, stability, and security.

Her mind wandered to another man who had earlier invaded her dreams. *I wonder if he wakes up cold and alone? Or does Sherry make his coffee too?*

Her back ached, unaccustomed to the hard plywood slab that served as her mattress. Muscles in her legs strained when she attempted to stand. "Ohhh, I don't think I moved an inch when I got back to sleep." She groaned, rubbing her calves and thighs. "There isn't a spot on me that doesn't hurt. I thought I was in shape, but I was wrong."

"You're in shape, all right." Mark laughed. "Just in the wrong spots. Hurry up with that coffee, will you? It's cold out here."

"Okay. Okay. I'm coming." It felt good to be with Mark again. Lauren was glad they were together, even if it was just for the summer.

Lauren searched the boxes, tins, and jars that lined the shelf above a three-burner propane stove, looking for matches. She finally found waterproof stick matches in the small pantry above the icebox. As Mark steered them through the middle of the narrow channel, she poured water into the aluminum coffeepot and lit the burner.

"It's awfully hard to boil water with this bumpy ride you're giving me."

Mark laughed. "It's awfully hard for you to boil water anywhere, Lauren. Don't blame me."

Surely no twins could be so different, yet so close. Their personalities, like their residences, were polar opposites. He loved to challenge the unknown. Boisterous, he liked being the center of attention. Lauren preferred quiet and routine. She loved her professional life in San Diego. Mark, on the other hand, shunned cities.

He had not only succeeded in staying alive and healthy, but had made friends throughout the world. Finding work had been easy for him with his many skills, likable personality, and easy manner. Lauren had accepted the accounting position at Metz's and had been advanced to senior accountant before she passed her CPA exam.

But it didn't make sense for them to live so far apart. When Mark left California three years ago, it had felt to Lauren that half of her was missing; as if a picture were torn in two. At least Mark had found a partner in Steve. Now, since her break with Richard, she didn't even have that.

Water boiled over the top of the little pot, hissing as it hit the burner. Lauren switched off the flame, tossed a spoonful of instant coffee into both of their mugs, and topped it with the scalding water. Balancing their coffee mugs in her hands, she stepped up to the main deck.

"Here you are, Captain." The brisk air took her breath away. "Oh, it is chilly out here. I thought it was just because I didn't have a jacket the last time I was out."

"Nice, huh?" Mark sipped his drink.

"Yeah, it's not so bad."

"Won't be long and we'll be in Naknek Bay. We'll put our net out there."

"What do you do? Throw the net over the side and scoop up the fish?"

"Yeah. Something like that. Actually, we lower the net off the stern—see that net over there?"

Lauren peered toward the rear of the boat. A large bundle of nylon netting with attached Styrofoam floats lay next to a huge fluorescent orange buoy.

"That's a gill net. We put it over the rollers and let it wheel as I pull away from it. There are lead sinkers on the bottom side of the net and cork floats on the top to keep it upright all the time. We lay out with our bow to the wind, and it trails behind us in a straight line."

"How do you know it's in a straight line?"

"Well, that's partly why we use that buoy. It serves as a marker for us, so we can keep track of where the net is— all hundred and fifty fathoms of it. But it's also got our name on it, and our Fish and Game number, so if the net becomes detached from the boat for some reason, they'll know who it belongs to."

"How long is a fathom?"

"Six feet to a fathom, so we've got about nine hundred feet."

Lauren whistled.

"That's the easy part," Mark explained. "The hard part is bringing it up."

"*We* haul it up? Doesn't that thing do all the work?" she asked, pointing at the metal contraption near the stern.

"Well, the winch helps pull it out of the water, but with a good catch, we could have as much as fifteen hundred pounds of salmon on the stern at any one time. We'll both be hooking them out of the net as fast as we can to distribute the weight."

Mark paused and slurped the cooling coffee. "That's why you need at least one partner on board. A full net might bring as much as ten tons. But I don't expect a catch like that. The *Ivy* couldn't hold it. We'd probably sink with that kind of weight on board."

"Ten tons?" Lauren gasped. "I wouldn't expect to see that many fish all summer."

"We may get that much in one fishing period. It won't take too long with both of us working at it—four, maybe five hours to unload the net."

"And what about the other net?" Lauren pointed at the nylon net that lay in the hold.

"That's the brailer. We hook that onto the crane when the scow comes alongside. We take the brailer off those securing hooks and attach it to their hook. They pick the salmon up with a crane and weigh it before they take it on board; then they dump the load, and give us back our net. It works real slick. Wait till you see it." The corners of Mark's eyes crinkled with his ever-ready grin.

She didn't mind that Mark found her naïveté amusing. Steve Buckner didn't think it was amusing at all. Her neck prickled as she recalled the lecture he had given her in the air. Unbidden, the vision of his tall, spruce-scented body as he helped her from the plane invaded her thoughts. Just the thought of him, warm and close, as he had been in her dream, halted the breath in her throat.

She would prove to him she knew how to work. "Just show me what to do, Mark. I can handle it."

"I know. That's why I asked you to come along. Free cook and shipmate, no lavish evenings in Anchorage, and best of all . . . you pay your own way."

"Mark, you rat." She playfully swatted his arm.

Three days passed quickly. Lauren brought some semblance of organization to their lives with prepared meals of chowder, stew, and vegetables served at consistent hours. For breakfast, grits or oatmeal were the usual fare. One morning she surprised Mark with melted cheese on English muffins. It was her way of civilizing her environment to a degree, amidst the roughness of his current lifestyle.

Buckner kept a close watch on his fishing interests, flying over the bay midmorning and late afternoon. Whenever Lauren heard the whine of his pontoon plane, her stomach churned. Her senses ran amok when she thought about him, his touch, his voice. She actually counted on those flybys, looking forward to seeing those wings dip and wave before he circled.

The extended daylight hours of Alaska's summer allowed more work time, and more work time allowed more time to think about her life. She was surprised that she thought more about Buckner than she did about Richard, even though she barely knew Mark's partner.

On their fifth night out, Mark threw down a losing poker hand and chuckled. "You and Steve ought to get together. Between the two of you, Las Vegas would be in shambles. I can't seem to beat either one of you."

"I wouldn't fly to Anchorage with him if I had a choice, much less Las Vegas," Lauren announced coldly. "I was just lucky. If he beats you at cards, I wouldn't be surprised to learn he'd cheated." Lauren felt her brother's gaze upon her, but she kept her eyes lowered, pretending a rabid interest in the cards she shuffled and reshuffled.

"So you don't think I should trust him, huh?"

"No, I don't."

"Why?"

Lauren wanted to say she would never trust a man who two-timed his women. She was sure Richard would never do that to her. It was obvious that Buckner was involved with Sherry. Yet, the way he drew Lauren against him . . .

"Maybe you don't know him as well as you think you do." Lauren squirmed. "I don't know. After I've had a look at your books I might have a better picture. I'll find out what I can. Maybe I'll discover there's nothing the matter, but till then, I'll follow my instincts. And right now, they point to him."

"Well, I happen to know him, and I trust him with my life. Yours too, for that matter."

"Because he's your partner?"

"And a good friend. You'll just have to get to know him."

"You asked for my opinion. I gave it." Lauren looked up. "Another game?"

"No, thanks. Let's get some sleep. It's up early again in the morning."

Lauren pondered her brother's suggestion, *Get to know him.* Was there more to Buckner than his rough manner and handsome exterior? In her mind's eye, she saw him as she had at the last, climbing into the Jeep, then smothered with a kiss from the attentive redhead. Lauren's stomach knotted. No. It was her brother who needed to know him better.

The next day, in spite of the overcast sky, the weather was balmy and warm. Opaque green water rocked the *Ivy* in a rhythmic lullaby while the sun played hide-and-seek, peeking in and out from the slow-moving haze above.

It had taken both of them a full three hours that morning to unload their catch. And it had been a good one. The stern was half-full of the prized king salmon.

"How're you doing, Lauren?"

She didn't bother to open her eyes. "Fine. I'm getting used to this lazy stuff. Maybe I'll change my mind about working for a living."

Mark laughed. "I'm tired. If you can take the watch, I'll go below." He checked the time. "It's two-thirty now. The tide is due to shift in two hours. Wake me up then, and we'll haul the net in."

"Okay." Lauren yawned and waved him aside. With her eyes closed, she mentally reviewed their morning's work— dropping the net, waiting, struggling to haul it aboard again, pulling the salmon out with the sharp gaff hook. Her shoulders and back still ached. Pulling in the heavily weighted net, even with the hydraulic winch, was hard work.

She stretched, stood up, and checked the position of the buoy bobbing softly in the distance.

With her twin below, Lauren again took up her position against the cabin, soaking up the scant sunshine that pierced through the haze.

A stiff breeze roused her. She glanced at her watch and realized, in horror, that it was five o'clock. She had been asleep. The boat had turned broadside to the wind.

"Mark. Get up here quick. Mark," she called again, seeing how dark the sky had become.

"What is it?" he answered from below.

"We're late. The tide's changed. We've drifted off course."

Mark bolted onto the deck and scoured the horizon for the corks and buoy marking the net's position. It had swept around the *Ivy* in a vast semicircle off the port side.

"What are we going to do?"

Mark ran to the bow and studied the waves that crashed nearby. "We've drifted too close to that sandbar. Quick! Pull up the net. I'll try to get us out of here."

Lauren threw the lever that activated the winch. She grabbed the thick rope net and strained to help the winch pull it from the water. Her shoulders throbbed with pain.

Mark started the engine, but as the big diesel ignited, the gill net jerked from Lauren's hands and jammed tight against the boat. The engine gurgled and died.

"What happened?" Lauren screamed.

"I don't know. The engine quit." Mark tried to start it again. It fired easily, but wouldn't grab.

"Mark—the net!"

Mark swore. "The net's in the propeller. We've got to get it out. Come on, Lauren. Pull!"

Together they strained to pull the net, but it wouldn't budge.

"We're drifting toward that bar. We've got to free the net!" Mark yelled above the crashing waves.

Lauren's heart pounded against her ribs as Steve's words repeated in her head. *Two brothers drowned in Bristol Bay. . . . It's no place for beginners.*

"Get a knife. Butcher knife," Mark commanded. "I'll keep trying to pull it."

Lauren ran to the kitchen, yanked the silverware drawer open, and sorted through the flatware. Under the butter knives, she finally found a butcher knife. Grabbing it, she ran back to Mark.

"It's all we have." She sawed furiously, but the blade was no match for the unyielding three-inch rope.

"Keep trying, Lauren. I'll get on the radio."

Her hands burned from the frigid water, becoming red and raw.

"Mayday! Mayday!" Mark shouted into the microphone.

Lauren could hear voices and static on the speaker; then Mark broke into their conversation again. "Mayday! Mayday! Dillingham *Ivy* in trouble! Come in, please."

Unconcerned laughter from the radio indicated that their message had not been received.

"Mayday!" Mark raised his voice again, then gave up. He took the knife from Lauren and hacked at the rope. "Try the radio, Lauren. Maybe someone will hear us." Lauren staggered past her brother.

"I can't believe it" Mark shouted. "It's the same spot those boys were in last week. We're going under."

The rim on the port side of the boat was now level with the icy water. Pushed over by enormous waves, the boat listed dangerously.

Mark continued to work on the unrelenting rope, while Lauren, fingers numb, stiffly switched channels and shouted the distress call. All at once, her ears filled with the sound of a small plane overhead. *Steve.* The mechanical drone kindled a spark of hope.

"Thank God," Mark shouted. "Lauren, take off your jacket. It's red—maybe they'll see us."

Lauren ripped at the strings that held her cumbersome life jacket in place.

The boat edged over the sandbar; relentless waves pushed it farther onto its side. They were taking on water.

Lauren shoved the scarlet jacket into her brother's frozen hands, and he waved it frantically above him. They both yelled for help, although they knew the pilot wouldn't hear them. Suddenly, the familiar silver-colored plane dropped below the mist. *Steve!* He was close enough to see them. Mark flagged the jacket back and forth.

The engine decelerated and the plane's wings dipped in acknowledgment, then began a slow, sweeping circle around the foundering boat.

"We'll be all right, Mark. Is he going to land?"

"I don't think so. The tide's too rough."

Lauren and Mark hugged each other, then continued to wave at the plane.

"I hope he knows we're in trouble and not just being friendly." Lauren's teeth chattered. Until now, she'd been unaware she was wet. Icy water had drenched her clothing, and the stiff breeze compounded the problem.

"I'm sure he could figure that out," Mark answered.

The tiny boat shuddered with each wave that pounded the exposed side, pushing them farther onto the bar. "We can't hold on much longer. I hope he sends help soon. Put the jacket back on, Lauren. And the life vest. That jacket will be awkward, but the insulation may help. If we go under before they get here, it'll make you easier to spot."

"We're not going under," Lauren stated. Her icy hands ached as she snapped on the down jacket. She could see her brother shivering, his T-shirt clinging like a second skin to his muscular frame. *Come on, Steve.* "I'll get your float coat and vest, Mark."

"We won't last fifteen minutes in the water."

He's right, she thought grimly. *We won't survive if help doesn't come soon.*

Another large wave pounded the side and pushed them off the bar, casting them adrift into the oceanbound tide.

At that moment the static-filled radio blared with fast-flying talk. "Dillingham *Ivy*—points off Naknek—Bristol Bay—"

"They're coming, Mark!" Lauren grasped her brother's arm.

His face looked stern, shadowed with guilt and shame. "I screwed up. I'm sorry, Lauren. The whole season ahead of us—gone."

Lauren looked at her twin, stunned. "You screwed up? *I* was the one who overslept. I was supposed to be standing watch."

"I shouldn't have left you out there. You were as tired as I was." He sighed dejectedly. "I guess Richard will be glad to see you. You'll be heading back to San Diego, right?"

Lauren's ire rose. "Admit he was right and I was wrong? I don't think so. I'm not walking out on you."

"I wouldn't blame you."

"I'm not giving up. If we—*when* we," she corrected, "land, we'll have that radio fixed and get back out here." She locked her gaze onto his face, demanding his full attention. "I promised to help you out this summer and I intend to do that."

The roar of a diesel engine interrupted them; then a second boat raced toward the *Ivy* from a distance. Mark waved at their rescuers. "Looks like we'll get that second chance, Lauren. Thanks. I'm going to hold you to it."

After some tricky maneuvers around the sandbar, a

young Eskimo fisherman pulled alongside and tied the *Ivy* to his boat with a thick jute line. After about an hour, they arrived at the Naknek Cannery dock. Mark and Lauren gratefully unloaded their catch from the net and gave the collection receipt to their rescuer as payment for the tow. It seemed a small compensation for their lives, but was well received.

The following morning, they found the *Ivy* beached high and dry beside the cannery pier. The tide was out. The dock Lauren had easily stepped onto last night was now at least twenty-five feet above the boat. Tall, oily wooden columns of the Naknek Cannery pier towered above them. It shocked her to see how severe the tides actually were. By afternoon, the beach they were sitting on would again disappear under twenty-five feet of churning, icy, Arctic water. She trembled when she realized how close they had come to dying in it.

Mark vaulted over the side onto the wet sand and walked to the stern to survey the damages. Feeling guilty about her role in the *Ivy*'s demise, Lauren clambered over the side and quietly followed him.

He reached under the brass propeller and pulled at the netting that was wedged against the shaft. With difficulty, he unwound a portion of the net and discovered a gaping hole. The heavy rope and netting had wedged itself into the hull as it chewed its way into the soft wood. Although it had caused the damage, it had also prevented water from entering the hold.

"Is it pretty bad, Mark?"

Her brother's mouth set into a grim line. "It's worse than I thought. Look at this." Mark shook his head in disbelief. "I'm surprised with the weight we had on we didn't go under."

"What can we do?"

"It's going to take a lot of work to fix this—two, three weeks. The propeller shaft is bent too. That's going to cost some money."

Lauren's mind began to churn. "What kind of jobs are available in Dillingham?" she asked.

"This was my only job," Mark muttered.

"No. I'm talking about for me."

"You want to go to work?"

"I'll make some money to keep us going while you get the boat fixed. How long did you say the season would last?"

"We've got a good five weeks left, maybe more. The humpies and silvers will run till August fifteenth, if we're lucky."

"Good. I'll get a job, and you fix the *Ivy* as soon as you can. Maybe we'll be able to get some fishing in yet."

"It's worth a try," Mark agreed. "Are you sure that's what you want to do?"

"Of course. Let's get to work."

They climbed the wooden dock ladder and had started toward the cannery when Lauren recognized a tall figure striding toward them. "Steve."

"Hey, Steve," Mark greeted his friend.

Lauren hung back, hoping to avoid the probing gray eyes.

"You two were lucky to get out of that one," Steve stated.

"I'll say." Mark shook his partner's hand. "You saved our lives."

"How are you doing, Lauren?" The deep voice vibrated the air between them and settled in her chest. Lauren's stomach tightened, and her hands suddenly dampened. She wanted to throw her arms around him and allow him to hold her, but knew better.

"Glad to be here. Thanks."

"You should have seen her, Steve. Calm as a trooper. Thank God she was with me. I wouldn't have made it without her."

"You might not have had the trouble if I hadn't been with you," Lauren admitted.

Steve removed a feather that had escaped her down jacket and found its way to her face. His hand brushed her cheek as he did. Her gaze joined with his, and she searched for meaning in his steady eyes.

"Come here, Steve," Mark interrupted. "You've got to see this."

Lauren watched as Steve followed Mark down the ladder to the crippled boat. She sat on the pier and waited for them. She still felt numb from the experience, as if it were a bad dream.

As they climbed back up, she heard Mark say, "It had to be sabotage, Steve. The radio worked when I installed it. The wire was cut."

Steve muttered something Lauren couldn't make out; then Mark replied, "I think I can handle it."

After the two men reached her perch and stood before Lauren, Mark asked Steve, "Would you be able to fly Lauren into Dillingham?"

"Sure. I'm leaving in about twenty minutes." His dark lashes hooded his eyes, and he seemed to be searching her face.

"Leaving us so soon?"

"I just need a ride into town," she said. "I didn't clean up the dishes or anything, Mark. I'm not really ready to go."

"Don't worry about it. I'll be here for quite a while, and I'll take care of the domestic chores."

"I'll meet you behind the cannery, Lauren. Twenty minutes." Steve slapped Mark on the back and left.

"What's with the radio?" Lauren asked.

"It worked after I had it repaired, and when I looked at it this morning, the transmitter wire was cut. That's why we could hear the radio and I thought it was all right. Steve couldn't get us to respond. That's why he kept checking on us."

A dark look crossed Mark's face. "I'm wondering about the anchor also. I was sure I had anchored securely, but it seemed I pulled up a pretty short line."

"You think someone wants you out of the way?"

"I don't know why. There's plenty out there for everyone." Mark shook his head.

"If you don't make your lease payment to Steve, I presume ownership would revert to him. Is that right?"

"I suppose technically, yes." Mark said. "But Steve wouldn't do that."

Lauren dropped her gaze.

"I know what you're thinking, Lauren. And I disagree. I don't think it's Steve."

"Who else stands to gain from your loss? Was he checking on us or his property?"

"I don't know. Here." Mark handed her a small key. "This will get you into the office. See what you can learn when you're in town. Maybe you can slip in at night. The computer on Sherry's desk isn't secured. You should be able to pull up the records without any problem."

"What am I looking for?"

"You know better than me. You're the accountant. Look for any large debts, double entries, whatever. My file is in Steve's office and would show the correct amount of my income and expenses with the *Ivy*. If the books are different, jot it down."

"Breaking into the office, Mark? Really."

"I don't think we need to be concerned, Lauren, but be careful." Mark hugged his twin. "Sorry I can't help you."

"Don't worry. Just get the radio and boat fixed and call me."

Lauren inhaled deeply in an effort to summon her courage. It did little, though. She had no job prospects, no contacts, and she would be separated from her brother in the middle of a wilderness state where her city instincts were virtually worthless. And now she found herself temporarily dependent on the one man whom she didn't trust. A cold hand gripped her heart as she realized that, like a pirate lying offshore in his ship, Steve was waiting.

Chapter Four

Steve adjusted his headset while Lauren crawled into the copilot's seat. The vibrations of the engines, as he warmed them, conveyed a sense of power and excitement in her. A week ago she had never flown in a small craft, but now she looked forward to soaring above the wild, rugged terrain and trees.

"Tighten up that seat belt, Lauren." Steve reached across to make sure her door was locked. His arm lightly brushed against her, searing with a pleasant white heat. "Can you get it?"

She tugged at the stiff webbing, then scrutinized the clasp.

"Here." Steve pulled the belt as far as it would go. "That should do it."

The belt tightened against her hips and pulled her back rigidly in the seat.

"That's kind of tight."

"We could loosen it if you want, but while we're in the air it would be better if you stayed on your own side of the cockpit."

"It's perfect," she shot back.

Steve's implication had a volatile effect. She quelled the eruption of feelings while he maneuvered the watercraft from the nearby cove.

"Scared?"

"No."

A dark lock fell across his high forehead, and dimples creased his otherwise masculine features. She resisted the urge to touch the close-trimmed beard to determine if it was as soft as it appeared.

"I thought you'd be packing to go home."

"And leave Mark? He's depending on the season for his income—as you well know. I couldn't let him down."

"Still in for those big Alaskan bucks, huh?"

"I traded one job for another this summer, that's all. I have to work for a living too."

"I figured a girl with your looks would latch onto the first moneymaker she could find and wing her way to an early wifely retirement."

"I don't depend on anyone to take care of me except myself."

"What about this?" Steve asked, lifting her left hand. "Doesn't your fiancé have anything to say about it?"

"Richard and I have an understanding. I have my own life to live."

"So you took his ring and gave him the slip, huh?"

"I didn't take anything from Richard. Ever."

The engine's steady whine filled the charged compartment.

Steve glanced at his passenger, then murmured, "Listen. I'm sorry. I guess I'm a little edgy."

Lauren's temper ebbed, but she kept her eyes fixed on the terrain below. "Me too. I shouldn't have said that. I really don't know you . . . but since you're Mark's partner, perhaps I should." *The sooner the better.* Although Mark didn't believe her, Buckner might be the culprit. For

Mark's sake, and hers, she would get to know this man. Mark had a boat, a stake, a partner to lose. She had an investment equally as valuable; she could lose her heart.

Buckner merely smiled.

Dillingham Bay came into view, then disappeared behind them. Lauren said nothing, thinking he had to approach the watery landing strip from a different angle, but the city faded in the distance.

"Where are we going?"

"I thought I'd take you past Aleknagik—a few miles north of here. You don't mind, do you?"

"I guess not, but don't you—"

"I don't have to be back until tomorrow," he interrupted.

"Well, I do. I've got to get back and look for a job."

"You won't be able to get anything done today. You deserve a little time off. I thought I'd show you something more of Alaska than the inside of a fishing boat."

"All night?"

Steve's face broke into a wry smile. "Did I say that? You're getting ahead of yourself, Lauren."

"Just take me home," she muttered.

"To my place?"

"Mine. The hotel, I mean."

"I know this great little place not far from here. Look." He pointed. "That little village down there is Aleknagik."

Lauren leaned forward to view the sleepy village nestled between tall standing spruce. Buildings emerged on either side of a river. "It's lovely. It looks like it's been painted there."

A small white building on the side of a hill stood crowned by an odd-shaped cross atop an onion-globe steeple. Several houses clustered along dirt roads, nestled in between tall spruce.

"You love it, don't you, Steve?"

"What?"

"Alaska."

"Yeah," he admitted. "That and flying. My two loves."
Lauren doubted that.

"Well, there may be more, but who's counting?" He
chuckled. "Actually, I need to check the propane tank at
my cabin. Like everything else I own, it seems to need
some attention. Here we are. Hold on, Lauren. We're going
down."

Lauren's eyes widened as Steve expertly maneuvered the
sturdy craft toward its watery landing strip. They glided
into the lake like a graceful bird, trailing a white foaming
wake behind them. He steered the plane into a sandy cove
where a lone cabin appeared from a clearing in front of a
dense spruce forest.

"There it is, home sweet home. Like it?"

"Well, yes, but—"

"But what?"

"Is it safe?"

"Safe from what?"

"Is it safe living out here alone like this? What if you
got hurt? Do you have a phone?"

"Are you expecting a native uprising?"

"No. But what about snakes? Bears? Prowlers?"

"Are you serious? There aren't any snakes up here; it's
too cold. And the bears . . ." He struggled to suppress his
laughter and take on a stern expression. "Don't worry
about the bears. If there are any around, I'll take care of
them. You have a wild imagination, Lauren. Maybe you
read too many books."

Lauren formed her words carefully. "I'm not in the habit
of making fun of others, Steve. And I don't appreciate it
coming from you, either."

"I haven't been making fun of you," Steve defended
himself. "I don't find you amusing." He closed the small

space between them. "In fact, that would be the last thing I would think of you."

His hand slipped unnoticed to the seat-belt latch; then she was vaguely aware of the click that released her from the strap. He slid his arm behind her and drew her closer to him. His mouth covered hers in a kiss before she could avert it, softly molding her lips to his.

When he released her and drew away, Lauren felt betrayed by her reciprocal response, embarrassed by her lack of restraint. He smoothed his fingers over hers until they stopped abruptly when they made contact with her ring.

"We shouldn't have done that," she said simply.

"I know. You seem to bring out the beast in me."

His words broke the spell he'd cast over her, and the redhead's image suddenly intruded. "You're a little free with your affections, aren't you?"

"I'm not the one wearing a ring, Lauren." A hurt expression colored his features; then he reached across Lauren to flip the door latch open. "C'mon. I've got to check that tank." When she hesitated, Steve held his hand out to her and said, "I'll be on my best behavior, I promise."

"All right . . . I just don't want you to get the idea that—"

"Forget it," Steve said in clipped tones. "I have my interests to protect."

Lauren digested Steve's retort. His interests—what interests did he have to protect that meant he couldn't mix business with personal relationships? Maybe his involvement with her would conflict with his plans to take over Mark's share of the partnership. Was that the only reason Steve drew back when she was more than willing to continue?

She stepped from the cockpit onto the dock, then waited while Steve moored the plane to a permanently attached rope. Lauren decided to overlook his unexpected kiss. It was obvious he already had.

If Buckner was behind the sabotage that could have cost them their lives, she had better keep her wits about her and insulate her heart. Aside from her belief that Steve was a womanizer, she had a job to do that required objectivity. She had to find out the truth about him quickly before it was too late for both her and Mark.

Inhaling deeply, she looked across miles of water to the vast wilderness that jointly encircled and isolated them. The water—dark gray and reflecting the overcast sky—looked ominous and forbidding, much like the water that had surrounded the boat when she and Mark dealt with disaster in Bristol Bay.

Steve's cabin, on the other hand, looked friendly and inviting. Well constructed and sturdy, it was made of smooth, short pieces of interlocking logs, stained with a natural oil to bring out the fresh-cut look, then varnished for protection against the harsh Alaskan winters. A generous layer of metal roofing capped it, giving the cabin a welcoming persona of its own; two sets of windows facing the west allowed an unobstructed view of the lake, and a single stovepipe emerged from the roof, promising wood heating of some sort.

Built on pole platforms, the cabin stood above ground and provided a large protected storage area underneath that housed a kayak, fuel tanks, and hand-split spruce logs. Large shaved logs comprised the three steps into the home.

The shore looked as if it stretched for miles in either direction, but was a short fifteen feet between the lake and the cabin. She bent and scooped a handful of dirt from the water's edge and let it sift through her fingers. Unlike the minute granulated sand of California beaches, this was an interesting combination of tiny pebbles mixed with wood chips and a mica-filled dirt.

"Great, isn't it?" Buckner asked.

"It really is beautiful. It's rugged. Quiet."

"That's one reason I like it here." His face softened. "Pure air. Water. No people. Beautiful country. Can't beat it." He fit a key into a large padlock and removed it from the metal hasp. "C'mon. I'll show you the rest of it."

He pushed the door open, and Lauren followed him inside. Colorful quilts adorned a set of bunk beds that lined the east wall. On the upper bunk was a patch quilt of elegant squares of velvet, wool, and old tweed, held together by a red feather-stitched thread. The lower bunk displayed a log-cabin design. Across the room, an antique double poster bed displayed a brightly appliquéd quilt of red apples. A kelly green border of lazy ribbonlike swirls connected each apple with a like-colored stem and leaf.

Brushing past the bed, Steve introduced Lauren to an antique potbellied stove. "This is Ironsides." Trimmed in shining chrome, it had lion's-paw feet and twin sliding doors that opened in the middle, and it looked like a comical deity that reigned against the north wall. Behind it, a solitary wooden mantel held an assortment of carved ivory objects and pieces of walrus tusk. A luxurious dark wool lambskin rug lay at Ironsides' feet.

A hand-hewn table and four spruce stump chairs occupied the space below the window, providing a gorgeous view of the lake. A long counter stretched the full length of the wall, displaying a portable four-burner stove and dozens of airtight containers of edible staples. There were no pictures on the well-insulated log walls, but the lack of additional adornment seemed wonderfully correct.

"My dad and I spent one summer building the whole cabin. We came back the next summer and made the furniture."

Lauren ran her hand over the smooth tabletop. "It looks like a lot of love went into your work."

"This is where I hide out," Steve confided.

"I can see why."

"Hungry?"

"A little."

"Me too. There's a pail in the corner. After I check out the tank, I'll start a fire in Ironsides. If you'll pick some blueberries, I'll whip up some batter."

"You planted blueberries?"

"They grow wild here—the biggest ones you've ever seen. You can get all you need within ten feet of the cabin, so don't go farther than that," he warned.

"Why?"

"Bears."

Steve gathered a handful of tools and stepped outside to the propane tank, while Lauren clomped down the log steps behind him.

It is nice here, she mused. *Quiet. Peaceful.* She plucked berries from chest-high bushes. Most of the blueberries were as big as her thumb and perfectly ripened. She popped some of the berries into her mouth, savoring the bittersweet taste.

It apparently hadn't taken Steve long to adjust the tank, for soon blue smoke blossomed from the stovepipe. In no time, Lauren had filled her bucket and returned to the cabin.

From the doorway, Steve eyed her openly. The stingy sunlight played peekaboo in the clouds, showering tiny sparks of light off her golden hair. She looked happy, self-absorbed, as she tried to lick blue stains from her fingers.

Lovely hands, he noticed. Long, slender fingers that belied their strength and sensitivity. His skin still tingled where she had trailed her fingers from his shoulders to his neck. His stomach tightened when he thought about it. *Hustling your partner's little sister . . . that takes some brains. What would Mark think? She sure knows how to raise my temperature. I wonder if that guy. Richard*—Steve shook his thoughts from his mind. *Don't blow it. Get control of yourself.*

Steve moved back, allowing Lauren inside. "I guess you were hungry." He grinned. "What are we going to do with all those blueberries?"

She looked at the bucketful of berries, then back at Steve. "Give them to Emily?"

"She'd like that," he said, taking the pail. "Ever made pan-fried muffins?"

"No."

"Help me clean these," he said. "I'll show you how."

When Lauren stood beside him at the sink, a whiff of spruce assailed her, and she spotted a fleck of bark on his shirt. She picked the piece of wood from his shirt, lifted it to her nose, and inhaled.

"When I met you I thought you were either a pirate, a Green Beret, or a deranged lumberjack kidnapping me from the airport."

"Which one did you settle on?"

Her green eyes glittered. "Pirate."

A satisfied smile stole over his features and lingered.

Silently, they picked out loose leaves and stems, then rinsed the berries and tossed some of the wild fruit into a creamy batter he'd prepared.

Later, when only crumbs remained of the muffins, Steve poured the last of the coffee and stretched out catlike in front of the ornate stove. Lauren perched on a stump chair, pleased to be elevated over her tall host for once. She did not want to compromise herself with this pirate, so she looked around the room, hoping to find a safe topic of conversation.

Her eyes fixed on the quilts, and she asked, "Where did you get those quilts? They're exquisite."

"Dad inherited the love apple quilt. I bought the other two at an antique auction in Portland. They came over on the first wagon trains into the Willamette Valley in Oregon.'' His smile broadened when he asked, ''Can you imagine sleeping under the very same blankets that pioneers did?''

''Well, I—''

He pursed his lips and sipped his coffee. ''Actually, I thought they fit rather well here—Alaska being our last frontier and all.''

''They are lovely.'' Lauren admired the intricacy, knowing it had required hundreds of hours of painstaking needlework for their completion.

''Why don't you join me?'' He smoothed his hand over the lambskin rug. ''It's more comfortable.''

Lauren denied the temptation to slide alongside him. It was hard for her to resist becoming another conquest among several, and he was the kind of man who would not be bound by love or honor. Of that she was sure.

''I told you—you're safe,'' he continued. She shook her head. ''What are your plans when you return to Dillingham?''

''I'm going to get a job. I don't know what's available, but I'll find something.''

''I can see it all now,'' he teased. ''Certified public accountant up to her elbows in soapy water at the local greasy spoon. Better yet, in the cannery, wading ankle-deep through fish guts—''

''I've done worse,'' Lauren interrupted. ''It wasn't the best pay, but I got by. And it's important that Mark gets up and running.''

Steve raised himself to a sitting position and stared into the flames.

Lauren studied his face. Did he regret whatever part he might have played in Mark's setback? Was she the variable he hadn't counted on when trying to rid himself of an unwanted partner? She wanted to remain objective while trying to prove Steve's guilt or innocence. She wanted with all her heart to believe he was not responsible for the trouble within the fleet, but if he wasn't, who was? Would the key Mark had secretly given her provide the information she needed to confirm or dispel her suspicions? His expression was a sad, sweet look that challenged her to trust him. The sharp smell of the spruce he'd stacked by the stove enveloped her now. It had a fresh, honest quality that stripped her of her defenses. Flames crackled and leaped in the stove as time hovered in a delicate balance of reality and fantasy. "I think we'd better go," Lauren said.

"Yeah. You're probably right, but we'll have to wait till the fire dies down. How about a walk outside?"

She expected resistance, anger, maybe resentment. Richard wouldn't have been so compliant. Never. Steve's response puzzled her.

He rose heavily from the floor and stretched his long legs as he stood. "By the way, Emily might have a job for you at the hotel."

"Doing what?"

"The native woman who does the cleaning is getting married, and Emily hasn't found a replacement. When she heard about the accident, she wondered if you'd be staying in Dillingham for a while, or heading back to California."

"That's great." Lauren paused. "Why did you wait until now to tell me?"

"I figured you'd be in a hurry to get right to work. After what you went through, you deserved a break—even if it was just a few hours. Besides"—his voice lowered huskily—"I wanted to get to know you better."

That's my line, she thought. She was not about to question him further. He seemed to be gentle, considerate, and loving. Lauren shook her head. She did not want to admit it, but despite her nagging suspicions, she found it difficult to believe that Buckner could be involved.

* * *

Although it was nearly ten o'clock at night, the sky was bright as midmorning when Emily greeted Lauren at the hotel entrance. Lauren welcomed the pillowy crush of Emily's embrace. In the older woman's arms she found refuge from the emotional storm that had built during the flight home. Her throat tightened as she tried to speak, choking the few words she meant to say.

Taking a deep breath, Lauren said, "Emily, I need a job."

"I was wondering if you'd be about, or if you'd be flying back home, dear."

"I'm staying, definitely," Lauren stated with a defiant lift of her chin. "I planned to help Mark out this summer, and I'm committed to do it." *I'd never go back now and face Richard's "I told you so." Whatever it takes, I'm going to stay.*

"Thatta girl," Emily said with a cheer. "You've got grit, I'll give you that much. Well, if you feel up to it, I need some temporary help cleaning rooms, changing linens— hotel maid work. I know it's not what you're used to—"

"I'll take it. I'll do a good job for you."

Emily's eyes reflected her approval. "I'm sure you will."

"Mark's going to fix the *Ivy* so we can finish the season. He'll let me know when it's ready. When can I start?"

"Don't worry about that now. I've got Maryann lined up until the end of the week—actually next Monday morning would work best for me. Can you find something to do between now and then?"

Lauren pondered that for a moment, a frown wrinkling her brow.

"What about all that reading you brought along?" Steve suggested.

Lauren shot him a disparaging glance.

"I've got a better idea," Steve started. "I'm flying back to Anchorage tomorrow morning. I've got business on the coast I need to take care of."

Emily and Lauren faced Steve, waiting for his suggestion.

"It wouldn't do to go alone," he stated.

"Oh, no," Lauren countered. "Don't even think about it."

"Steven's right, Lauren. No one should fly out alone under any conditions. It's much safer to have at least two people aboard a plane. My Max always insisted."

"But you were married," Lauren protested. "We're—"

"Steven wouldn't compromise you, would you, Steven?"

Steve vigorously shook his head.

"But Mark—"

"We'll call Mark and leave word at the cannery," Steve interrupted. "That's a good idea."

A little apprehensive, a little excited, Lauren resigned herself to going along for the ride. "Where will we be going?"

"Anchorage, Juneau, Ketchikan. It'll give you a chance to see the Alaskan coast while you're here."

Emily fairly danced. "What a wonderful idea, Steven," she said, clapping her hands together. To Lauren she said, "You really should, Lauren. You'll have a wonderful time."

You're sure? she wanted to say. Emily's eyes twinkled as if it were *she* who was invited.

"This will be perfect. I'll look for you two by Friday evening. Steven, you take good care of her now. I feel some responsibility here," Emily cautioned.

"No problem, Emmie. I feel safer already knowing Lauren will be aboard."

Lauren's brow furrowed. She couldn't be sure how she

felt about this sudden turn of events, but she felt as if she'd been had.

Emily gave the girl a reassuring hug. "Take some pictures for me, will you, dear? It's been years since I've visited the coast."

"Sure, I'll do that."

"You brought a camera, didn't you?" Emily asked.

"Yes, I have one of those autofocus, autoflash things. It even takes panorama."

Emily squeezed Lauren's arm and giggled. "Oh, good. We'll have fun looking over your pictures when you get back."

"What do I need to bring in the way of clothing?" Lauren asked Steve.

"Same things you're wearing. You don't need much."

Lauren rolled her eyes. Men were so useless when it came to clothes. When Lauren had spoken to Mark before her trip he had told her to bring jeans, tennis shoes, and a sweatshirt or two. She had brought all that and more.

"Swimsuit, if you have one," Steve advised.

"Why a swimsuit?"

"We might have a chance to kayak in Ketchikan. The water's warm there."

"Really?" Lauren asked, surprised. "It's not all business, then?"

"Not entirely. I'd like to leave by six-thirty or seven. Can you be ready?"

"I'm almost ready now."

"Good."

Steve dialed the Naknek Cannery number and asked the operator there to leave a message for Mark Cole. He waited patiently on the line, and then gave the message to someone who assured him that Mark would receive it. He leaned over and kissed Emily's waiting cheek. "We'll see you later, Emmie."

Steve left abruptly, and the two women were left feeling as if they had been surrounded then dropped by an evasive whirlwind.

"Things happen fast around here, don't they?" Lauren asked the older woman.

"Certainly with Steven they do." Emily chuckled. "You run along and have a good time, now. He's a good boy. He'll take care of you, I promise." Emily winked at her and then pretended concern. "If he doesn't, now"—she wagged a motherly finger at Lauren—"I want to know."

"The girl's back."

"Yeah, I heard. So what happened to her brother?"

"Licking his wounds, I guess. I woulda thought that little incident woulda sent 'em both hightailin' back to the lower forty."

"Lucky for you it wasn't worse."

"Me? You're in this as deep as I am, clown. How'd I know the punk was going to cooperate? Nearly signed his own death warrant."

"Nature takes its course."

"I won't be no part to killin'."

"We didn't do anything. We just helped out a little."

"I don't like it. Why don't we just cash in with what we got and lay low?"

"Like you said, Marin. We're in this together." Index finger tapping out an unmistakable message onto Marin's chest, the man in the shadows emphasized his final words. "Don't forget it."

Chapter Five

That night, Lauren packed her things in a small weekend bag, then added her camera and a couple rolls of film. The following day she waited in the lobby and watched for Steve. It was sunny outside, but the idea of flying to Anchorage and beyond still made her a little nervous.

Steve arrived shortly, and after Lauren tossed her bag into the back of his Jeep and clambered aboard, they were off, kicking up gravel and dust in front of the Briarwood as he shifted between first and second.

They parked behind the Dillingham Air office in a grassy area, and Lauren followed Steve to his plane. He climbed onto the wing and stowed his bag, then reached back for Lauren's. After he tucked it behind her seat, he offered his hand to her.

''Need help?''

She took his outstretched hand and easily hoisted herself onto the wing beside him. She slid into the passenger seat, and Steve latched the door for her. He leaped off the wing and strolled behind the plane to enter from his side.

Lauren watched, fascinated this time, as he pulled on his headphones, then attended to the numerous dials and switches before he ignited the engine. He listened carefully to the sounds that his engines made as they started and warmed. Steve tried different idles and listened closely before he requested permission to taxi, then take off from Dillingham's airfield.

Pressed back in her seat as they accelerated skyward, Lauren leaned slightly to her right and watched as they surged over the treetops and began a slow circle high above the airstrip. Steve deliberately flew southward, then veered north over the city, dipping his wings over Emily's hotel. Soon the city lay far behind them as Steve nosed his craft toward Lake Clark Pass.

"How do you feel?" Steve asked her when the plane had leveled off.

"Fine." Lauren nodded. "It's pretty out here."

Steve pushed a button on the dash, and the small cab filled with a New Age instrumental. A woman's haunting voice wound among the stringed instruments as the soothing piece filled their compartment.

"That's nice, Steve. I wouldn't have thought you liked that kind of music."

Steve nodded. "I like it."

They soared high over the ranges, and Steve named them for Lauren, pointing out ancient lava flows, cinder mountains, lakes, and streams.

Lake Clark Pass was a veritable palette of artist's colors as the minerals, rocks, and slides caught the morning sun's rays. About a half mile away a small plane heading toward Dillingham intercepted Steve's radio frequency, and Lauren caught Steve's one-sided conversation.

They flew on toward Anchorage, and in another hour, Lauren was surprised to see the massive peak of Mount McKinley rising in the distance.

"Boy, it's clear today," Steve noted. "Good visibility all the way in."

"Is it usually cloudy?"

"We rarely get a day like this. Must be our lucky day."

His conversation eased Lauren, and she felt more comfortable with him this morning than she had at any time previous. *I won't let that distract me, though,* she told herself. She would be on the alert for anything unusual she might detect about Steve. It wouldn't do to take him at face value until the truth about the mishaps was finally resolved, if at all.

Steve broke into her thoughts once more as he reached Merrill Field's frequency and requested permission to land at the municipal airport. Permission granted, Steve followed the course prescribed and began their descent toward the landing strip. He taxied his plane in front of the same hangar and parked it very near where he and Lauren had picked it up earlier that week. Had it been only days? It seemed so much longer.

When he had shut down the engines, Steve left the cockpit and hopped onto the cement. Lauren struggled with her seat belt, then unlocked her door and flipped the latch handle, allowing the door to pop open. Her tennis shoes afforded her better traction on the wing than the sandals she had worn previously, so she declined Steve's offer to help her down.

The two of them walked toward Duke Reilly's bay at the Alyeska hangar. Steve removed his sunglasses as they entered the darkened hangar, and Lauren followed suit.

"Buckner!" Duke shouted. "Hey, buddy . . . back so soon?" The two men shook hands.

"Lauren, right?" Duke nodded at her, wiping his greasy hands on a rag he whipped from his back pocket. He wore the same baseball cap and gray-striped overalls, which looked like they hadn't seen the inside of a washing machine since the last time she had seen Mark's friend.

"Hi, Duke."

"You back so soon? Where's Mark?"

"On the boat," Steve replied. "Had a little problem outside Naknek."

Duke's brow furrowed, and he looked concerned. "What happened? Is he okay?"

"Mark's fine," Steve assured him. "The boat's a little worse for wear, though. We'll be down a few weeks, looks like."

"Deliberate?" Duke queried.

"Part of it. Maybe. But there's another little matter I want to speak to you about. Mind if we go in the office?"

"Sure. Fine."

"Lauren, there's a ladies' room and lounge right next to the office. Coke machines and stuff. If you don't mind waiting, I won't be long."

"Okay." Lauren shrugged. "I'll stretch my legs." Before she turned to find the lounge, she watched the two retreat to Duke's office and shut the door behind them. Lauren wished for just a moment that she could have stayed with them. Although it seemed none of her business, it concerned her that the conversation might include information about the possible sabotage that Steve had alluded to. She had no one to call, although she wished she could have spoken to Mark in person before this trip. Even a word to Emily would help make her feel a little less detached and alone. She settled into a low-slung fabric chair that hung suspended on a chrome frame.

Steve and Duke talked for close to ten minutes before Lauren began feeling a little edgy. The wall was penetrable to the degree that she heard a few words, like *scramble, radio, fleet*, and a curse, before she heard a noise that sounded like a fist connecting with Duke's desk. Duke's voice remained at an even, steady tone throughout. Suddenly the door to Duke's office opened and Lauren jumped.

"I'll leave it with you till we get back, then."

''Right. I'll take every inch of that line apart and check the electrical—top to bottom,'' Duke replied.

''Looks like we're going to change planes, Lauren,'' Steve announced when the two men entered the room. ''Duke's got a float plane here that we'll lease to take south.''

''Yeah?'' Lauren was surprised. ''Is there a problem with yours?''

''I want Duke to check it out thoroughly before we take it back. This way he'll have a few days to work on it for me.''

Duke shook his head. ''Just as well you're off the boat. Sounds like Mark's had his share of problems with that.''

''Steve told you.'' It was a statement rather than a question. Lauren confirmed it had been part of their conversation.

Duke nodded. ''I told that brother of yours to stay away from boats and women—uh, sorry 'bout that, miss. I mean I told him to watch his backside—aw shucks. Just never mind.''

Lauren chuckled at Duke's apparent attempt at polite conversation that was ill suited for mixed company. She glanced at Steve and saw him grinning as well.

''I'd check with the two outfits we talked about,'' Duke addressed Steve. ''Bet you'll find what you're looking for.''

The two men shook hands. ''Okay. Where's this plane we're talking about?'' Steve asked.

Duke swung himself into the driver's side of a golf-cart contraption. ''Hop in,'' he invited. ''We'll get your gear and I'll take you over there.''

They drove to Steve's plane, unloaded their bags, and Steve pocketed a couple of items from his stowage compartment, then reboarded the little cart. Duke swung it around and headed toward what appeared to be the back of the hangar. The airstrip paralleled a protected cove where the float planes were moored. About 150 planes were currently tied down, bobbing softly in the water.

Duke pointed out a green float plane. ''A de Havilland Beaver. That's the little beauty right there.''

''Is it ready to go?'' Steve asked.

''I checked it in myself. Everything's a go.''

''OK, Reilly. We'll see you sometime Thursday or Friday. Before midday,'' he added.

''Fine. You've got my number if you need to reach me before then.''

''Right.''

''See you, miss.''

''Thanks, Duke. We'll see you soon.''

Duke adjusted his oily baseball cap, put the little cart in gear, and sputtered away.

''Funny guy,'' Lauren said, as he disappeared in front of the hangar.

''Yeah. You make him nervous.''

''Me?''

''Women in general.'' Steve grinned. ''I told you, He's a confirmed bachelor.''

''There's a reason for that,'' Lauren concluded.

Steve adjusted the seat to accommodate his six-foot-plus height, then fixed the mirrors—right, left, and rear—before donning his headset. He acquainted himself with the instrumentation before he started the engines and let them idle, then he motored the craft backward and out of the watery slip.

He connected with the flight control center, and soon they were airborne.

After they had made their departure from Anchorage airspace, Lauren asked, ''Are you going to tell me where we're going?''

''Details,'' Steve responded.

"Small, but important," she coaxed.

"We should make Juneau this afternoon."

"What's there?"

"Business. You'll have plenty to do while I'm busy; then tomorrow morning we'll head on down the coast."

"To?" Lauren probed.

"Possibly Sitka. For sure Ketchikan."

"Business there too?"

"Mostly. I've got a friend who owns a cabin in Ketchikan Bay. We'll stay there."

"In the bay?"

"An island in the bay. It's very nice."

"Is he married? Got a family?"

"Nope to both. Are you interested?"

"You're presumptuous." *Impossible. Incorrigible.*

"Curiosity killed the cat, they say."

"I just like knowing where I'm going," Lauren countered. "I don't think that's unreasonable."

Steve chuckled. "You must've been a cute kid with that little pout of yours. I'll bet you got anything you wanted."

"I wish."

"We'll be flying along the coast for quite a while," he said. "If you're tired you should rest now before things get interesting."

"Thanks."

Steve extracted his CD from a breast pocket of his jacket and punched the plane's CD player. "Put your headset on."

"You brought it along?" Lauren eyed him with an appreciative glance.

"You liked it."

"Yes," she murmured. "I did."

He shoved the disc in, and immediately a low, soft sound emerged.

"That's nice, Steve. Thank you."

"I'll wake you when there's something to see."

Lauren snuggled against the pillow she made of her rolled-up sweatshirt. "Okay."

When she awakened sometime later, Lauren sensed that a large block of time had passed. The terrain below looked like nothing she had encountered on the trips to and from Anchorage.

"Where are we?"

"According to my calculations we should be passing over Yakutat Bay soon."

She checked her watch. They had been flying for close to three hours. "Boy, I conked out, didn't I?"

"These long days and short nights can throw you off."

"You probably think sleeping's all I do."

"You're all right." Steve's deep voice vibrated the air when he chuckled. "You look so sweet when you're asleep."

"Only when I'm sleeping, huh?"

"No comment."

"Noncommittal, Buckner?"

"Yep."

Steve followed the coastline south, and soon the water opened up into a large, protected bay. The hills that lined the coast were free of roads and buildings and looked untouched by man. Various islands dotted the inlets and appeared to be little mounds of trees growing straight up out of the water.

"Right below Yakutat is Glacier Bay. I'm going to take it lower so you can get a look." He banked the plane to the right, reducing altitude, and leveled off about a thousand feet above the tree line.

"Are those white things in the water ice?"

"Icebergs, to be exact. We're almost there. Glacier Bay is a national park now. There are several glaciers here. It's awesome to watch the ice floes calving—huge chunks of ice break off and collapse into the bay.''

Inside their aircraft Lauren thought she heard a muffled boom. ''What was that?''

''The Indians called it White Thunder.'' You can see the ice collapse; the water starts to boil and roll, and you can hear the thunder as the sound travels.''

''Oh, my,'' Lauren whispered. ''Take me closer, can you?'' She pressed her face to the window like a child at a toy store and watched for another calving.

''Like I said, it's awesome.''

Several small boats that conducted tours of Glacier Bay were in the area as Steve buzzed over the top of them. Passengers waved, and Steve dipped his wings in acknowledgment.

Lauren watched, fascinated, as they skimmed over the top of the icy floes. Great fingers of ice jutted from the earth, white and turquoise in color, separated from the solid floe beneath.

''I see one, Steve.'' Lauren watched as columns of ice plummeted down and collapsed into the pewter blue water. Immediately the water began its roll outward, and Lauren heard the muffled thunder. ''It's better in person than in the movies,'' she declared. ''It's unbelievable.''

''We're not too far out now. We'll be in Juneau within the hour.''

''It's been a long flight, Steve. Are you tired?''

''Nah. I'd be steering a boat, or in a Jeep, if I wasn't flying. No difference.''

The skies surrounding Alaska's capital looked overcast, and they flew through a bank of fog. It was a muted sky, unlike the bright blue sunny sky they had enjoyed en route to Anchorage. As they crested the top of one more hill, Juneau's outlying houses and buildings came into view.

Steve circled out over the water and approached the city from the south, following his tower instructions.

When they landed, Steve taxied the float plane to a city dock, where planes were allowed to moor. They hailed a water taxi, and Steve asked the driver for directions to the Port Authority offices. When they reached the dock, Steve handed the bags up to Lauren, paid the fee, and retrieved a ticket for his plane.

"Just like a parking lot," Lauren noted.

Steve tucked the ticket into his wallet. "Yep. Just like back home parking your car." He hooked a thumb into the loop of his daypack and stepped onto the sidewalk.

Juneau spared no expense with the potted plants that decorated the city streets. The downtown area looked as well groomed as San Diego's wharf area. The streets were mildly busy with what looked like local traffic intermingled with tour buses and shuttles.

Steve hailed a taxi. "I'll get you settled in the hotel. Then I'll be gone for a few hours. There's plenty to do."

"What would you suggest?"

"Wander downtown if you like. There are museums, saloons, shopping. Or if you'd rather, take a taxi to the Mendenhall Glacier. It's a short ride just north of town."

"A real glacier?"

"Yeah. It's pretty neat. Juneau's the only city in Alaska that has its own glacier."

The taxi stopped in front of the old Juneau hotel downtown. Steve booked them in separate but adjoining rooms, and Lauren was unaware of when he left.

As he suggested, she took the taxi to Mendenhall and told the driver not to wait. She joined other tourists at the bottom of the trail, awed by the massive ice floe that stretched in view of the parking lot. Armed with her camera, Lauren started up the path that wound up about three-quarters of a mile around the mountain base. One of the

first park signs she saw warned about the dangers of en-
countering a bear on the trail: BEAR COUNTRY. Inscribed
on the sign was a paw print that extended well beyond
Lauren's outstretched fingers: five toes and equally long
claw prints. *Avoid Confrontation,* it warned. *No problem,*
Lauren thought. *I'm not looking for one. Odors Attract
Bears.* Lauren raised her shoulder and sniffed her collar for
any remaining perfume that might have lingered since the
last time she had worn the windbreaker. *Hike During Daylight Hours, in Groups When Possible.* Lauren paid attention to that one and sidled up to the closest group and
walked a comfortable distance behind them.

The leaves of the trees that lined the trail were wet from
a light rain that had fallen earlier. The earth smelled moist
and rich, thick with underbrush and spruce trees and what
looked like an indigenous maple. Every turn on the trail
revealed a new angle of the glacier. The ice floe looked
immense and impenetrable. In the quiet she could almost
hear the groan and crunch of the floe as it moved its massive weight westward.

Lauren took pictures at several intervals before she
reached the top of the trail and a busy visitors' center.
Juneau's sky was overcast, as was the sky as far west as
she could see. Layers of mist hung on the surrounding hills
that held the glacier in their arms like a sleeping giant.
Turquoise veins of color similar to those she had seen in
Glacier Bay marbled the ice. Mendenhall flowed down into
a river that would carry its contents to the sea.

At the visitors' center, Lauren dialed the number on the
card her driver had given her and asked for a taxi to meet
her at the parking lot below the glacier trail.

When she reached the hotel, Steve had apparently returned. She heard him rustling about in the suite next door.
After she had taken a shower and changed clothes she rang
his room. They would meet for dinner in ten minutes.

*   *   *

Steve and Lauren meandered the streets of Juneau before deciding on a restaurant. On a back street, they strolled past St. Nicholas, the oldest active Russian Orthodox church in Alaska. Built in 1894, its onion-globe top, painted a pale gold, perched atop the well-maintained white frame church. They continued past numerous brick structures couched between frame houses, apartments, log homes, and commercial stores.

Finally, Steve took her into the Red Dog Saloon—vintage 1776. The inside walls and ceiling held a veritable treasure of souvenirs left by the early inhabitants of the area—evidence they had been there. The two claimed a table near the bar, where Lauren could get a good look at the entire two-story saloon.

Steve settled on a Red Dog burger and beer, while Lauren decided to try a fish entrée. Afterward, they continued their walk down the length of the business district, then sat on a cedar bench and watched the tourists file by.

''Seems like a big industry here, Steve.''

''Tourism?'' He stretched back against the bench and crossed his long legs at the ankles. ''Yeah. That and fishing. Juneau used to have the biggest hard-rock gold mining operation in the state in the early days.''

''How is it you know so much about Juneau?''

''I spent a summer here with a buddy of mine, Frank Tomlinson.'' He chuckled. ''We had some wild times that summer.''

''Like?''

''Do you remember seeing a bridge on the left as you headed toward Mendenhall?''

Lauren thought for a moment, then recalled the bridge that crossed the river. ''Yes. A little north of here.''

''One night after we'd been working all day and spent a few hours at a local pub, Frank and his friends—there were six of us—decided to jump off the bridge into the water—about a hundred feet down.''

''Why would you—''

''There was a guy we called Domino who had done everything a human could possibly do and live to tell about it. Or so he said. He claimed he had jumped from that bridge before, so we decided to try it.''

Lauren rolled her eyes. Six grown men—or what should have been. She shook her head.

''We all counted down, and four of us jumped in. Frank waited for Domino to make his move, and when he didn't he grabbed Domino's shirt, and the two of them came down after us.''

''Cold?'' she asked.

''You bet!''

''And so . . .''

''We were fools. I admit it.''

''And have you jumped off any bridges lately?''

''Not lately.'' Steve grinned. ''I think I've earned my degree in stupidity. We were young. Dumb.''

''We all do things we regret,'' Lauren countered. ''Some of us are lucky enough to live through it.''

''Conditions up here don't allow for much foolishness, unfortunately. It still is very much a state where the strong survive.''

''Were you able to finish your business here?''

''Yep. Tomorrow we'll fly to Ketchikan. It's not too far away. I've got some business to tend to there, and then we'll look up my friend.''

''Frank Tomlinson?''

''No. A guy named Bill Peters. His family goes a long way back in Ketchikan.''

''Frank doesn't live here anymore?''

''We lost touch years ago. I think he moved back to the lower forty—Portland or somewhere.''

Steve slapped his hand on his thigh and abruptly stood up. "Guess we ought to call it a day. I want to leave fairly early tomorrow."

"What time?"

"No later than six-fifteen. Need me to get you up?"

"I'll call the desk for a wake-up. I'll be ready."

Lauren had trouble falling asleep that night and blamed it on the long nap she'd taken on the ride over. Steve's story about his summer in Juneau left her curious, though. Why did he and his father decide to settle in Dillingham, rather than in one of the more developed cities like Juneau or Anchorage? What was the attraction to that remote northern location? What became of the rest of Steve's friends?

The next morning, bolstered by a shower and coffee, Lauren felt ready to meet the day. They flew out of Juneau into more misty skies, and although it was hard for her to gauge their direction by the muted sun, the coastline indicated they were flying south. Steve paralleled the Inside Passage of Alaska's southeast coast. It wasn't much more than two hours before they descended into the sleepy village of Ketchikan.

A very large logging operation occupied a section of Ketchikan's cove. But it appeared that the industry here was split between logging, crabbing and fishing, cruise ship tourism, and locals who catered to all.

They tied down very near the business district and found a restaurant, aptly named the Last Chance Café. It was obviously a locals' favorite, a few crusty looking customers lingered over coffee and newspapers, acknowledging the newcomers with a cursory glance and nod.

Red-checkered vinyl tablecloths covered each of the three-by-three tables in the small café, looking as if they had not been removed or replaced for years. A dark-haired, bearded, large-bellied cook could be seen behind the counter, which held an assortment of coffeepots, shake machines, stoneware, and other kitchen accessories. The café seemed to have been built on an old pier, as the floor appeared to be highly varnished planks of the original dock. In all, it was a homey, colorful welcome to this very old fishing village.

"Coffee, you two?" the waitress hollered.

"Black," Steve replied, answering for both of them.

"Be right with you."

The menus, laminated sheets of colored paper, were jammed between the salt and pepper shakers that sat in a chrome basket.

The waitress brought their coffee, steaming, in thick stoneware mugs and set them between Steve and Lauren. "What can I bring you two? Are you hungry this morning?"

"Starved," Steve boomed. "Skinny here will probably need something too."

The waitress, a petite, fuzzy-haired blond, pulled a pencil from behind her ear and smiled at Lauren. "You let this big guy talk about you like that?" she said, jerking her pencil in Steve's direction.

"It makes him feel important," Lauren joked with her budding conspirator. "Men are like that, you know."

"Do I ever." She tapped her pencil on the pad. "What d'ya say, big guy? What'll ya have?"

"A little sugar with that humble pie you're serving me, and the Loggerhead Special."

"Right. And you, Skinny?" She smiled at Lauren.

"Two eggs, scrambled well, toast, and coffee."

"Keep the coffee coming," Steve added.

"Gotcha." The waitress ripped her ticket from the pad and slipped it under the chrome clip, twirling the slip to face the cook, then waited on another table.

"So. What are you doing here today, Steve? Or should I ask?"

"Same as yesterday. I won't be long."

"None of my business, apparently."

"Nothing you'd be interested in."

Lauren wished she could follow him and learn for herself why he was being so secretive about his business. It was not enough to observe him as he dealt with people. Steve seemed equally comfortable with the lofty and the lowly. He was private about his business, but seemed open with his relationships. It intrigued her.

"Looks like we'll have nice weather today and tomorrow. I've got a surprise for you. I think you'll enjoy it." Steve sipped his coffee.

"We're not bridge diving today, are we?"

"No. After I'm through here, we'll take the plane over to Bill's house and see if we can scare him up."

"Should we phone him first?"

Steve laughed. "Last I knew he didn't have electricity or phone service on his island. It's pretty primitive, but nice."

The waitress filled their mugs once and soon returned with their breakfast. She set a large slice of apple pie in front of Steve and set his Alaskan-size breakfast to the side. "Humble pie and one Loggerhead," she said, winking at Lauren. "And a little something for Skinny."

Lauren laughed along with Steve. "You make a guy feel right at home, ma'am," Steve said. A hint of red tinged the sharp planes of his cheeks visible above his beard.

The little blond circled her arm around Steve's large shoulders and gave him a squeeze. "Pie's on me, big guy. Eat up, you two. I'll be back with more coffee."

Steve left a large tip under his plate when they were through. Shouting his thanks to the cook, he hoisted a thumbs-up sign. The waitress shooed them out with her hand towel and wished them a good day. Lauren left the café with more than their meal as they stepped out onto Ketchikan's main street.

"Why don't you check in with Emily?" Steve suggested. "See if she's heard from Mark. I've got to call the office and put out any fires there."

Sherry's fire, no doubt. Lauren took the phone card from Steve and dialed Emily's number. Emily had not heard from Mark, and everything was quiet as far as she knew. Lauren let her know they were in Ketchikan and would probably be heading back in a day or two. Emily urged Lauren again to take lots of pictures and said she looked for their return Friday evening.

Steve seemed somber after his phone call, but didn't share the nature of his conversation with Lauren. He left her to wander the streets of Ketchikan while he tended to business, pointing her in the direction of the historic Creek Street district that was now gift shops and city-maintained landmarks.

Lauren shot pictures of the old buildings, once brothels, perched atop high-water stilts that remained in good repair after over a hundred years. Most of the houses, she discovered, were designed with a trapdoor built into the living room floor—used for bootlegging deliveries during the Prohibition years, and possibly for fishing from the safety of one's own living room. She learned that Ketchikan had very little snowfall, but boasted the highest level of rain in the state—over one hundred and fifty inches per year, and their days were, more often than not, blessed with liquid sunshine.

Steve caught up with her around 10:30 and escorted her back to the little Mooney. "All set?" he asked after they had strapped in. "We're outta here."

They motored the craft out of the bay and lifted off,

skimming low over the water. "We're not going too far," he explained. "Bill lives about four miles out of town."

Within minutes, Steve recognized Bill's island and swooped down toward it, making a full circle around the house. It truly was a small island, complete with stately spruce and a log home that appeared to have been built fairly recently. "Boat's gone," Steve announced.

"He's not home?"

"Doesn't look like it."

"Is that a problem?"

"No. I know where he keeps a key," Steve said, "if he bothered to lock it."

He eased the float plane down on the north side of the island, where Bill had secured a floating log dock. After he had cut the engine, he steered the little craft alongside the dock and tied it to one of the large iron securing rings. Steve stepped onto the dock and reached in to help Lauren.

They were met on land by a large, black, shaggy-haired collie that barked a warning in time to its wagging tail. "Hallie!" Steve called. "Come here, girl." The dog acted confused, cocking its head back and forth as it approached the pair, no longer barking.

"Good girl." Steve allowed the dog to sniff his hand, then scratched her head gently between the ears.

Hallie eyed Steve's female companion and stood still while Lauren cautiously held her hand out for inspection.

"Hallie's a good girl, isn't she?" Steve addressed the dog. "Where's Bill, Hallie? Is he working today?" The big dog bounded in front of them and led them toward the house, tail wagging vigorously high above its back.

Steve knocked on the handmade wooden door, and pushed it open when no one answered. "Bill?" It was evident that Bill had gone for the day. Dishes lay soaking in the sink, and the coffeepot yielded warm grounds in the filtered reservoir. "He'll be back," Steve deduced. "Looks like he hasn't been gone long."

Lauren looked around the large one-room main floor and peered up at the bedroom loft above. She jumped as an outdoor generator kicked in and battered the otherwise still air.

"I see he's installed a generator, anyway. Probably got some hot water now too." Steve turned the faucet on and confirmed he had. "What'd I tell you?" he asked Lauren. "Nice, huh?"

"Very. He keeps it up pretty well for being a bachelor."

"Let's get our things. We've got lots of daylight left. We'll go have some fun."

Lauren followed him down the sturdy log steps. Hallie, having decided they were all right, flanked Lauren and kept in step with her new human friend. Large tail wagging, the dog seemed happy to have the company.

"Looks like you found a friend."

"She's a pretty girl," Lauren said, stroking her hand down the dog's back. Hallie sat down abruptly and raised a right paw. "Oh, I don't have anything to give you, girl." She patted the dog's head. "Come on, let's see if we can find something."

Lauren headed back toward the house, and Hallie skipped forward, bent to pick up a stick in her mouth, and ran ahead. "Come on, girl. Give me the stick." The dog bounded forward, raising her face to Lauren's with the stick clamped firmly in her teeth. She obediently dropped it in front of Lauren and backed up, swaying her big hind end as she reversed. "Good girl." Lauren scooped up the stick, drew back, and threw it several yards away toward the water's edge. Hallie fetched the stick and jauntily returned to Lauren. "I think I started something here," Lauren shouted to Steve. He gathered their bags and took them into Bill's house.

After a few minutes of playing with the dog, Lauren joined Steve in the house. "So what's up?"

"I thought we'd hang around here today and wait for Bill. Tomorrow we'll head down to the Misty Fjords, about twenty-five miles south of here. But for now, let's go swimming. Bill's got a kayak on the side of the house, if you want to use it. We might as well have some fun while we're waiting for him."

"Sure," Lauren agreed. "I'll be right with you." She donned her swimsuit, a sensible one-piece navy blue Lycra, and jogged down to the dock, where Steve was entertaining Hallie. Steve took her hand and led her into the water.

"It's warm," she cried out, surprised. "You didn't tell me—this is warmer than San Diego."

When he had waded in waist-high, Steve dived in and paddled out into the channel. "Come on, Lauren."

She dived in and headed toward Steve. To her surprise, Hallie bounded into the water behind her and swam toward them. "Will she be all right?"

"Seems to be. We'll stay close to the beach, okay?"

Hallie dog-paddled around them, but soon tired of the sport and headed toward the beach. She shook her coat vigorously, then began barking at the swimmers.

"I think she's worried about us."

"She'll be okay, Lauren. I'll race you to the dock."

Before long, they heard an outboard motor approaching. The pilot eased his boat next to the dock and leaped out to secure it. Steve waded out of the water and toweled off to greet his friend.

"Well, I'll be. Steve!" Bill recognized him. "Man, it's good to see you."

Bill and Steve embraced as two old friends and then parted and shook hands in the more traditional manly fashion. "You old son of a gun," Bill shouted, slapping him on the back. "Good to see you, buddy." At the same time, he glanced at Lauren and grinned. "Who's this lucky lady?"

"My partner's sister, Lauren."

Bill pumped her hand vigorously, shaking her whole body as he did so. Lauren immediately liked Bill Peters.

"Come on in, you guys. What a great surprise!"

After taking turns in the shower, Lauren and Steve were served Bill's homemade chili. He was pleased to learn they'd be sharing his home for the evening. As Steve had assured her, Bill was thrilled with their company and was not shy about letting them know it.

Lauren decided that Bill was of worthy character and that he held Steve in high regard. She felt sheepish and more than a little self-conscious that she could have suspected anything less of Steve—unless there was something so deep it was hidden from everyone's view. But even now, her female intuition told her he was above reproach.

Steve and Bill talked long into the night after Bill fashioned Lauren a bed on the couch with a sleeping bag Steve provided. She heard them mention names of their mutual friends, but no one she recognized. Hours later, Lauren was vaguely aware that the men had finished their six-pack of beer and decided to call it a night.

After a big breakfast of pancakes and orange juice, Bill helped Steve tie the two-man kayak onto the Mooney.

"I wish I was going with you," he said. "But you guys have a good time. I'll have supper on when you get back tonight."

Lauren and Steve shoved off after Bill left, trailing a wake of white foam behind him. Steve seemed familiar with the terrain and flew them to the mouth of the state park. "This is the most awesome place on earth," he said when they landed.

Lauren eagerly looked forward to what Steve seemed to

think was no less than heaven on earth. Steve had opted to wear only a T-shirt over his swimsuit, so when he secured the plane with a long line to the trunk of a towering spruce, Lauren peeled off her shoes, socks, and jeans in the cramped compartment. Wearing a sweatshirt over her swimsuit, she slipped into the water that reached midthigh on her.

Steve pulled two paddles from the belly of the kayak and laid them on the pebbly beach. He stuffed their food and extra clothes into a dry sack and shoved it deep into the front of the kayak. Lauren joined him on the shore and peered all around the cove. A thick green moss covered the trees heavily on the north face of their trunks, and the underbrush was thick and wild.

"Misty Fjords is a rain forest. You wouldn't believe it here in Alaska, would you?" he asked.

"It's beautiful!"

"You haven't seen anything yet. Here." He handed her a paddle. "First a little kayak lesson."

Lauren's imagination took over, and Steve was her shipwrecked captain, cautioning her about the dangers of this uninhabited island. His long legs, well shaped and muscular, glistened in the muted sunlight. She would not have minded taking lessons from the likes of him, anywhere.

Steve seemed to sense that her mind was elsewhere and fixed a sobering glare on her.

"I'm listening." She grinned, back in the present.

He showed her how to fix her thumbs and fingers on the paddle to lessen wrist strain and possible injury. "You'll be up front, so you'll do most of the steering," he told her. "I'll provide most of the push."

Lauren liked the sound of that. As usual, it seemed Steve was looking out for her. Lesson over, she climbed in, pulled a baseball cap low onto her forehead, and adjusted her sunglasses.

"Ready?" When Lauren nodded, Steve leveraged his paddle and pushed them away from shore, and they began a southward journey into the Misty Fjords.

"Just take it slow, Lauren," Steve cautioned. "Left, right, left, right." Soon they paddled in unison, and even though she didn't have the same reach that Buckner had with his long arms, Lauren did her share to keep the kayak headed in the direction Steve wanted them to go.

Twenty minutes into the fjord, they came upon a raging waterfall that jutted seemingly straight out of the hill above them. The water surged and crashed, becoming a beautiful cascade into the channel. On a quiet shore beyond, Lauren spotted a crested white heron standing as still as a statue.

Lauren yanked at the strap around her neck and hauled the camera up out of her sweatshirt. "I've got to take some pictures. Will you hold it steady, Steve?"

Silently, Steve rested his paddle in front of him and steadied the little craft. A family of sea otters raced and rolled not far from their bow, and Lauren braced her paddle with her elbows as she snapped pictures, hoping not to scare them. Steve steered them closer, silently dipping his paddle and occasionally resting it in front of him.

Steve was right. It was incredible. Lovely. Captivating. She wanted to go on this way forever.

"If we're lucky," Steve murmured, "we'll see some bears along the shore."

"Really?"

"Sure."

"They won't come out here, will they?"

"Not unless you invite them." He chuckled. "They feed along the shore. They don't need to swim for it."

At that moment a bald eagle swooped down in front of them and snagged a fish. Flapping its huge wings, the graceful bird rose with its prey hooked in golden claws.

"Oh, Steve, I can't believe this."

"Can't say I've ever seen one so close," Steve remarked. "We're getting quite a show today."

Steve and Lauren paddled past sheer black cliffs of what looked like granite. Mist rose from their base, layering the channel in an enchanting fog.

"It's like we've traveled back in time," Lauren whispered. "I'd never even heard of this place."

"Few people have. It's so inaccessible, it will never be overrun with outsiders."

She laughed at a cluster of pudgy white birds with exotic-looking faces and beaks, fluttering on a high ledge. Other than the slap of the paddles and the gentle lapping of waves upon an occasional shore, the birds were the most significant sounds they heard. Shrouded by layers of moving fog, the peaks of the fjords alternately appeared and disappeared around each bend.

"This channel stretches one hundred miles south," Steve told her. "I've not been down all the way, but I will someday."

"I'd love to come back here with Mark," Lauren mused. "Has he been here?"

"Not that I know of."

It seemed hours had passed when Steve decided they had ventured far enough and should turn around. Lauren checked her watch. It was nearing four o'clock. "I can't believe it. The whole day has gone by."

"They say once you've seen Alaska you never go all the way home."

Lauren was sure of it. Everything she had seen today had proven that.

If only she felt this sure about every aspect of Steven Buckner. She felt so at ease with him—almost as comfortable and unencumbered as she did with her twin. "Can we bring Mark down here sometime?" Lauren asked impulsively. "I'd like to see the whole thing."

"We could camp out here. There are plenty of sites along the shore," Steve suggested.

"But the bears!"

"They won't bother you if you leave 'em alone."

"But don't they go after food and stuff?"

"They like fish. I wouldn't bring bacon, eggs, or steak out here, but dried fruit, crackers, cheese, and things like that won't arouse too much attention."

Lauren sighed. "I am getting tired. It's been so much fun, Steve."

"We'll head back. I'm sure Bill will be there soon."

A couple of hours later they reached the Beaver. As before, Steve beached the kayak and they stretched, revived themselves with the snacks he'd brought along, and began to prepare the kayak for the trip back to Bill's island.

Lauren looked back wistfully as Steve took them above the mists and the shrouded channel and rose above Misty Fjords. She felt as if she were leaving a warm, loving place.

When Steve shut down the engine of the float plane, they could hear the generator yammering in the distance like a jackhammer. Hallie bounded down to the dock, greeting them with a welcoming bark this time. Lauren saw Bill open the door to his home and step onto the porch.

They spent the evening playing an aggressive game of Monopoly that lasted several hours. The two men seemed to enjoy just having the time together to relax. Hallie lay at Lauren's feet, appearing to enjoy the attention Lauren gave her.

Reluctantly, Bill saw them to the dock early the next day. Lauren received a big Alaskan bear hug from the mountain of a man, with a promise that they would return soon and spend more time. Steve asked his friend to visit if he made it up north, and the two parted with a handshake. Lauren thought Bill looked lonely as they revved the engines and lifted off.

Chapter Six

They made good time and landed in Anchorage about 4:30 that afternoon. Duke had an extensive list of items he had checked out and replaced on Steve's Mooney. Lauren gathered that he had found nothing worthy of alarm. She couldn't help but feel that Duke made a great effort to avoid speaking to her. After Steve had settled the bill with Duke and paid for the deHavilland, they left for Dillingham.

Lauren let Emily know when they had returned. After the tiring daylong trip, Steve wanted to get home and had dropped Lauren off at the Briarwood.

Emily and Lauren agreed on a starting time Monday and decided to meet that morning. Lauren had a couple of days to rest.

Before she left for breakfast Monday morning, Lauren was paged to the front desk for a phone call.

"Lauren, can you hear me?"

Lauren listened on the static-filled receiver. "Mark?"

"Can you hear me?"

"Where are you calling from?"

"Ship-to-shore phone."

"It's a little scratchy, Mark, but go ahead."

"I'm glad you're back. Did you have a good time?"

"Yes." *That trip has given me memories to last my lifetime.* "What's going on with the boat?"

"It's coming along. Got lots to do yet. Listen, I've been talking to some other owners who've had some weird things going on. Did you get a look in the office yet?"

Lauren's moist hand involuntarily clutched the receiver tighter against her cheek. "No."

"Do it. Tonight, if you can."

"I'll try, Mark."

"Be careful," Mark cautioned. "I'll call again tomorrow."

Mark signed off; then Lauren replaced the phone in its cradle. She had a job today, a mission tonight. She had to get going. After the past few days she had spent with Steve, Lauren wanted to believe he was far removed from their bout of bad luck, but they needed to be sure. With that in mind, she pushed all conflicting thoughts of Steve Buckner aside. After a light breakfast, she hurried to join Emily in the lobby.

"Isn't it a beautiful day, Lauren?"

She hadn't noticed until now, but it was nice outside. The usual haze had not yet arrived, and warm sunlight flooded the room.

"Your job starts with cleaning the lobby, hallways, and community facilities before the guests get up. By ten o'clock you start on individual rooms as they become vacant. The overnighters are supposed to be out by eleven. I'll check back with you at ten and show you how we make the beds."

Lauren took up the tools of her trade and set upon the lobby. She could see that certain spots had, for a long time, been ignored.

Wouldn't Richard love to see me now, she thought, *working as a hotel maid.* Envisioning the smug expression she guessed he would wear, Lauren attacked the cobwebs that hung on the high curtain rods with a renewed fury, as if she could wipe away the imaginary I-told-you-so smirk from his face.

By 9:30, Lauren had done as much as she could until the rooms were vacant. Her thoughts, this time, focused on Mark's elusive partner. His smiling image swam before her: a little-boy innocence behind the dimples, hard work in the becoming tan, honesty in those gray eyes. She closed her eyes and willed the vision to cease, but it would not leave her completely.

"Ready to clean rooms, Lauren?" Emily's cheery voice broke into her daydream.

While they worked, Emily chatted about the happenings inside Dillingham—who was going out, and the government men who would be coming in.

"How well do you know Steve?" Lauren asked impulsively.

"Steven?" A curious frown wrinkled Emily's forehead for an instant. "Since he was about waist-high." Emily gauged his height with her hand against her middle. "He'd been coming up for the summers with his father for years. Max knew his dad real well, and we kinda adopted them. He's grown up around me, I guess." She sighed heavily. "Max and I never had kids of our own. So I've been more than a mother to Steven. He moved up here permanent after his father died. He was raised in California. Had a wife for a while." Emily sighed. "Poor thing."

"What do you mean? He wasn't abusive?"

She clucked her tongue. "Oh, no. Nothing like that. He seemed good to her and all, but she just didn't like it here. She only lasted about three weeks. They divorced shortly after that."

Lauren exhaled, unaware that she'd been holding her breath.

"What was she like?"

"She was a stewardess. Pretty thing." Emily bent over the bed to straighten a crease. "But I know she wasn't happy."

"Monogrammed luggage, right?"

"Why, yes. I believe she did have monograms on her suitcases."

Lauren imagined that the luggage Steve's ex-wife carried had held a showcase of the latest fashions and designer labels that he accused Lauren of packing. *No wonder he thought—*

Emily plumped a pillow, then grabbed another. "I think it kind of soured Steven on life for a while. Then he lost his father."

That Steve lost two people he loved may have been the impetus that spurred a shadowed life. Lauren felt her brows furrow as she contemplated this information.

"Did Steven behave around you?"

"Oh, yes. He was the perfect gentleman. There's just something I can't put my finger on."

"I know what you mean." Emily pondered for a moment. "He's been through a lot, and I think he puts up quite a wall when there's a female around. I could be wrong."

Very wrong, if Sherry is an indicator. "He's very reserved around me."

"Steven quit flying full-time a couple of years ago, and bought out most of the private boats and formed a fleet. The fishermen sure needed some organization."

"Is he trying to form a monopoly?" Greed would certainly color a man's judgment as far as the lengths he would attempt to go to destroy competition.

"No . . . Most of the local fishermen didn't have the

means to maintain their boats and equipment as they should have. If anything, Steven salvaged their incomes instead of taking advantage of them.''

Lauren's expression must have sparked a different meaning in Emily's eyes as she continued, ''Steven would make any woman a good catch. I know Sherry Mallory's had her eye on him for quite a while . . . can't say I blame her.'' Emily chuckled, and her whole body shook. ''He's a good boy.''

Lauren smiled at her new friend's observation, even though it struck a little too close to home for her. Steve Buckner would be a handsome catch, if a woman was hunting a husband.

''I'm sure Sherry's heard by now, there's a new girl in town,'' Emily added.

''I met her.''

''She's very pretty.''

''I understand she lives with her father.''

Emily nodded. ''So I hear. I don't know what he does for a living. Never could figure that out. He has his own money, I know that. But I don't know from what. Some seem to think he's come into it. Could be just talk. You know how small towns are.''

Lauren nodded in agreement, although she had always lived in a metropolis and knew nothing of how small towns really were.

''Kinda keeps to himself and hasn't made any friends to speak of.''

''He doesn't work?''

''Nothing I can think of. He's kinda like a go-between for different outfits, setting things up and the like, but I don't think he really works at anything.''

''Hmmm.'' Lauren wondered how this information might help her. If she could slip into the office tonight as

Mark had asked, perhaps that might shed some light on any dealings the elder Mallory might have with Steve.

Each room took about twelve minutes to clean, and with Emily's friendly conversation, the time passed quickly.

All at once Lauren sensed, rather than saw, an unnerving energy behind her. She turned to see the figure of a large man looming in the doorway.

"Why, Steven," Emily gushed. "Your ears must be ringing. We were just talking about you."

"Oh, yeah? What could you two possibly find interesting about me?"

"Not a thing." Emily chuckled. "What are you doing here? I thought you'd be out keeping track of the fleet today."

"Just came to check on my favorite girl," he teased. "And to talk you out of a piece of your pie. Got any around?"

"Steven, for you, anything. You bring Lauren up in just a minute and I'll warm some of that blueberry pie I made for you."

Steve winked at Lauren. "I knew she'd put all those berries to good use."

Lauren's eyes lowered when she realized how she was dressed. She pulled a flowered bandanna from her unruly curls, and rubbed the tops of her stained leather tennis shoes on the calves of her tight-fitting jeans.

Steve watched her as she modestly gripped the bottom of the oversize T-shirt that billowed around her hips.

"You'd have to catch me looking like this, wouldn't you?"

Steve's face broke into a wide smile.

"Don't say it, Buckner."

"What? I like it." Gray eyes met green. "It suits you, L. C. C'mon. Let's go get some pie."

She led the way up the narrow staircase to Emily's apartment, consummately aware of Steve's disturbing presence behind her.

"Did you miss me?"

"After four days with you I should miss you?" she asked tartly.

As she grasped the doorknob, his hand closed over hers. The touch sent tremors racing through her. Her heart quickened. He stood scant inches away from her in the small space. He was so close she could feel the heat emanating between them. So close she felt as if he were stealing the air meant for her to breathe. For just a moment, Lauren allowed herself the luxury of wondering how it would feel to be in his arms again, how his lips would feel crushing against hers, how he would taste.

He grinned smugly, as if he knew the maddening effect he had on her. "Allow me," he said, turning the knob.

The door opened into an airy room bathed in sunlight that swept the disturbing feelings away. Fuchsia and African violets lined the windowsill, basking in a warm southern exposure behind double-paned glass. The whole upstairs apartment seemed softly warmed by the heat from large bay windows. The smell of fresh-baked blueberry pie permeated the room with a homey sweetness.

Lauren glanced around her. A highly waxed oak floor mirrored scant furnishings. On top of a wide bookcase, an old portable record player—flanked by two speakers— guarded the corner. In front of it, a faded rag rug was the only covering on the floor.

Lauren's eyes strayed to the gleaming surface of an electric organ that stood next to the bookcase. A tiny ornate gilt frame—the only object that graced the organ—housed a black-and-white snapshot of an older man wearing coveralls, standing beside a dark-haired man and child in front of an airplane. The boy looked to be nine or ten, an intent glare on his young face. The man, obviously his father from his look-alike features, grinned broadly. A black lock fell over his forehead, giving him a roguish appearance that Lauren recognized. Lauren moved closer to look.

"That's Max, my father, and me," Steve said.

"Nice-looking man," she commented. *Looks just like you.*

Steve claimed a chrome-legged kitchen chair. "How about that pie, Emmie?"

"Right after lunch, Steven. You know better than to have dessert before lunch in my house." Emily set a sandwich of thick-sliced ham down in front of Steve and another in front of Lauren.

"Eat up, now. I'm warming the pie."

"I've been thinking about blueberry pie all morning." Steve winked at Lauren.

"You must've smelled it from the street."

He chuckled. "Smelled good too."

Emily brought two dessert plates to the table, heaped with steaming blueberry pie. "Try that on for size."

Lauren's eyes widened at the huge portions Emily had dished out.

"Eat up, Skinny," he ordered Lauren. Playfully tugging on her T-shirt, he teased, "Look at this, Emmie. Nothing but skin and bones."

"You're one to talk, Steven. I'll bet you're still living on peanut butter sandwiches."

"Only when I'm in a hurry," he admitted. "The rest of the time I forage for handouts from you." Patting his stomach, he continued, "You can see I'm not suffering."

"Well, you keep coming over, and I'll keep trying my recipes out on you," Emily offered. "Make sure they're fit for human consumption."

"Lauren wouldn't believe I'm qualified to express a human opinion, would you, Lauren?"

"I plead the fifth."

Steve's banter with Emily was another facet of him Lauren hadn't seen before. It was obvious he was fond of the older woman. Again she wondered if this man could possibly engage in criminal or scurrilous activities.

After coffee, Steve stretched his arms above his head and yawned. "I've got to see Randy in Bethel this afternoon."

"When are you leaving?" Emily asked.

"About four o'clock. I'll be back first thing in the morning."

Good. Lauren felt relieved. *He'll be out of the way.*

"I told Randy you might come with me, Lauren. He knows Mark and wanted to meet you. He said if you're a bookkeeper he'd like to ask you something about taxes. Wanna come along?"

Emily answered for her. "Of course she would."

"I don't think so," Lauren objected. "I've got work to do, and I—"

"Steven said he'd be back before work tomorrow, so there's no reason why you shouldn't," Emily countered. "I've got a jar of salmonberries for Ruth. You can take those to her, can't you, Steven?"

"Of course I will. No problem."

How can I get out of this? Mark's going to call in the morning. "I'm sorry," Lauren insisted. "I'd like to go but I'm expecting Mark to call. I shouldn't miss it."

"You won't, I'll have you back early," Steve promised.

"You go on, Lauren, and don't think another thing about it," Emily encouraged her.

Lauren glanced at Steve from the corner of her eye. The satisfied grin he wore bespoke victory. He appeared ready to burst out laughing. Noisily, he shoved his chair back and stood, leaning over the table to plant a kiss on Emily's waiting cheek. "I'll be back around four, Emmie."

Lauren watched him leave. When the door closed behind

him, she felt the vibrancy in the room dissipate, returning it to the peaceful aura that was uniquely Emily's.

While clearing the table, Lauren wondered about Steve's motives. *Why does he want me to go with him? Is he trying to get me away from Dillingham, or just get me alone? Who is Randy? And does he really want to meet me?*

There were too many inconsistencies. Steve's preoccupation with business, yet his seeming disdain of it; his harsh exterior that collided with the softness he displayed around Emily. His apparent gentleness with Lauren; yet his permissiveness with Sherry.

This trip to Bethel might provide some answers, or at least some clues. Steve's friend, Randy, might prove to be helpful. Although being alone again with Steve set her up for personal heartache or risk, she might discover some answers to questions she had.

Around four o'clock, Steve arrived in an open-cab Jeep. He eyed Lauren and said, "You look worried. Why?"

"You're a glutton for punishment, aren't you?"

"How's that?"

"I thought you'd had enough of me these past few days."

"Let's just say I enjoy your company."

Lauren shrugged. His answer was safe enough. "Okay."

The look in his eyes told her that if she had any sense she should be worried. Worried about the way her emotions ran wild when she was around him. Worried about wanting to look good for this man. Worried she would fail in the mission Mark had given her.

Steve carefully loaded the salmonberries into the back of the Jeep, then ceremoniously deposited Lauren's satchel beside them.

As they drove through town, Lauren saw a shabbily dressed man leaning against a tavern wall. She smiled at him, but the man's dour expression didn't change. He reminded her of the many homeless vagrants that loitered around the wharves of old San Diego—waiting for handouts and odd jobs to keep them in whiskey. She tried to shake off the chill that settled upon her under the man's gaze.

"You okay?"

"Yeah. Sure. I'm fine." Determined to leave unpleasantness behind, she savored the wild rush of air that swept her hair back. "How long does it take to get to Bethel?" Lauren made a comb of her fingers and drew a wayward hair from her face.

Buckner liked the contrasting pink from her cheeks that glowed near the dark blue sweater she wore. "About as long as we want it to take."

"An hour? Two? Three?"

"Twenty minutes by air." Buckner was accustomed to seeing a lot of beautiful women in California: suntanned, healthy, lean, and leggy. But Lauren topped them all. *Does she know what it does to me when she sets her mouth just so, with that delectable little pout she wears when she knows she's been had?*

He hated to put himself through this kind of sweet torture—being so close to her. *Why does she still wear Richard's ring? How do I stand a chance against an invisible adversary?*

Lauren closed her eyes, yet she could still see Steve's handsome, smiling face. When she opened her eyes, she found that her mind was uncannily correct. He looked the same in person as he did inside her head. Gorgeous. It was impossible to quell the attraction she felt for him. Unlike her unemotional attitude toward the man she would have married, she fought to keep her feelings reined around Buckner. The refreshing wind that tore past her seemed to strip her inhibitions away as well. *You're crazy, girl,* she berated herself.

All too soon, they reached the hangar and pulled their gear from the back of the Jeep. Lauren helped load their baggage, and they climbed aboard his plane. Within minutes, they were in the air. As Steve banked the gleaming Mooney toward Bethel, Dillingham vanished.

After a brief fifteen minutes flying over trees and tundra, they landed at Bethel's airstrip. Steve secured the plane to a tie-down, then off-loaded the supplies. Randy Scott arrived in the North Star Lodge van to shuttle his guests from the strip. He obviously held Steve in high regard, his young eyes noting every detail of his appearance before his gaze swept to Steve's female companion.

"This is Lauren," was Steve's introduction. "The bookkeeper."

Calling Lauren a bookkeeper was like calling a certified chef a short-order cook, but Lauren graciously extended her hand to Randy.

"Hard to imagine you're related to Mark. I'm pleased to meet you, Lauren."

Randy seemed as open and honest as anyone Lauren had ever encountered. He was the epitome of the boy everyone wanted their daughter to marry: wholesome, fresh faced, and sincere.

"Been flying much, Steve?" Randy asked when they had started down the road.

"All the time. I've been really busy this season—hardly have any free time at all—but I'm not complaining."

"Yeah." Randy glanced in the rearview mirror at Lauren and smiled. "I can understand that. How's my Minnow?"

"Doing great. Miller's making quite a haul, and your boat is the fastest in the fleet, so he'll do well for you. I brought your check."

"I appreciate that, Steve."

"Well, you don't seem to get down our way too often, so I thought I'd make the trip for you."

"You're the best, Buckner."

Randy's friendliness instantly set her at ease and caused her momentary shame. It would be inconceivable for anyone to suspect this "apple pie" young man of conspiracy to do harm to anyone or anything. A stream of freckles showered his flawless skin and set the stage for his large blue eyes. The only crime Randy might be found guilty of was making people feel good around him. He was a natural PR man.

The thicket of trees opened into a wide, lush meadow. Instead of being a rustic lodge somewhat on the order of Buckner's cabin, the North Star Lodge stood two stories high, and looked like an alpine manor. Guarded by tall spruce sentinels, and surrounded by the forest on three sides, the lodge commanded a breathtaking view of a glacial lake that opened into a wide, crystal expanse of sapphire blue.

"Randy, it's beautiful!"

The young man beamed. "Everyone says that when they see it the first time. It accommodates thirty guests."

White gingerbread trim edged the eaves of the huge A-frame. A decorative fence with cutout designs, typical of alpine Europe, bordered the spacious wooden porch that encircled the building.

"I designed it and had it built," Randy explained, "with logs cleared from the property." He pointed out the vast area of land that had been cleared. "All this used to be forest."

"Do you live here year-round?" Lauren asked.

"Ruth does, my manager. I leave before Labor Day for the university. I'm studying architecture. I make it back here for Christmas and spring break, and Ruth usually takes a trip south sometime in between."

"Just wait till Ruth sees who we brought home for dinner," Steve teased. "Another skinny mainlander."

"Yeah." Randy chuckled. "She's going to like that."

Mrs. Perry seemed genuinely pleased with her new guests. Ruth was a wiry, middle-aged sprite with fading auburn hair.

"Got your salmonberries, Ruth," Steve said, lifting the jar from the back of the van.

"Great. We didn't get many this year. Just take them into the kitchen for me. I promised our guests we'd have a special treat this week."

As they made their way into the lodge, Randy said, "Make yourself at home, you two. Lauren, Ruth made up the guest room for you. Steve, you can have your regular bunk."

Opening a wide, handmade door, Randy led the way inside an airy, open-beamed lobby. A fire, already stoked in the floor-to-ceiling rock fireplace, lent an added coziness to the room. In front of it sat a seven-foot leather couch flanked by matching wing-back chairs. A large brown bear rug completed the effect of rustic elegance.

Lauren turned full circle, admiring it all. "It's just so beautiful," she said. "I'm overwhelmed."

"Thanks. I love it here. It's been my life's work, so far," Randy said.

"We serve dinner at seven o'clock," Ruth announced, "so you've got time to explore."

"Steve said you had a couple of tax questions you wanted to ask me, Randy. Is that right?"

"If it's no trouble. I had some questions on the percentage of deductions allowed and a couple of other little things on my Schedule E."

"Sure, I'll go over it with you."

After Lauren stowed her things in her room, Randy met her in the lobby and guided her to a small office at the rear of the lodge. He asked her a few pertinent questions about his business. They discussed contract labor versus employees, commercial rental income information, and other concerns. Randy took notes on the information she provided.

"You've been a great help, Lauren. My trouble is that I'm not so good at this. Ruth's great with the cooking and the customers. . . . Me . . . I'm a fledgling architect, not an accountant. I could use some tax advice now and then."

"Hey, no problem. When I get my business set up you're welcome to call me anytime. I'll help you any way I can."

After their meeting, Lauren strolled through the meadow and down to the lakeshore. Water lapped gently onto the gravel where she knelt and swirled her fingers in the icy waves. Looking around she spied a grassy knoll where she could bask in the sunshine. The lake was serene and wide. A turquoise sky hosted a few capricious clouds that danced across its sunlit stage.

She leaned back on her elbows and raised her face to the sun; the light and heat felt rapturous upon her skin. *This has got to be heaven.*

A small distance away, two people squealed and laughed as they reeled a fish into their dinghy. "Another big one," she heard one shout. Lauren shifted her arms to cradle her head, then closed her eyes. It felt good just to relax, unhurried, letting her cares and concerns slip away.

What seemed a short time later, a loud, clear bell announcing the dinner hour roused Lauren. A feast that spanned the length of the banquet table awaited her and the others. The noisy guests tried to outdo each other's stories of fishing and hunting escapades.

Having eaten all she could comfortably hold, Lauren declined a high-capped chocolate pie and left the gregarious group to sit in the adjoining room in front of the fire. She drew her feet beneath her and stared vacantly into the scarlet flames.

Steve's electric presence surrounded her, and a comforting warmth permeated her body as he sat beside her on the couch.

"I thought I'd find you here." His low voice vibrated the air between them.

Lauren smiled.

"What'd I tell you?" Steve patted his full stomach. "Ruth cooks a spread like this every night. Keeps her guests fat and happy."

"I can see why they love to come here. I would love to just eat and sleep, watch the sun go down and the stars come out, and sleep some more."

She peered into his face as Steve edged closer, his black lashes forming a lovely fan over his dusky gray irises, and watched the reflection of the flames dance in his eyes.

"Ummm . . ." Raising her fingers to his lips, he kissed them lightly. "Sounds like a good idea. I know just the place. . . ."

"I'm sure you do, Buckner." She playfully nudged her shoulder into his chest, too aware of the woodsy male scent that was uniquely his. She knew she could not resist the handsome pilot if she allowed his closeness to affect her. . . .

Steve stood suddenly and pulled Lauren up with him. "Let's go outside." He seemed unaware of the physical effect he had on her. He looked cool and unaffected, so sure of himself. "Come on," he whispered.

Clearing her throat, Ruth stopped Steve in his tracks. "And where is it you two think you're going?" Giggles and knowing glances from the guests who lingered in the dining room punctuated her question.

"Just going to check the grounds for bears, Ruth. Excuse us, folks."

Laughter erupted from the table.

"You go right ahead, Steven. I know I can always rely on you to have my guests' best interests in mind." Turning to her company, she asked, "Who's ready for a game of cards?"

Lauren did not resist the strong hand clamped on her wrist, but followed Steve through the front door.

"I've never been so embarrassed. They all think we're ... uh, you know."

"They were just having fun. You notice I protected your virtue."

"Is that what you call it? It looks to me like I'm going to leave here a marked woman."

"Do you want to go back?"

"Well, it's a little chilly, Steve. Don't you think we should get our coats?"

"And lose a good excuse to warm you in my arms? Not a chance."

His answer secretly pleased Lauren, and, for the moment, she decided to follow her heart. "I can't believe I'm doing this."

Steve pulled Lauren close. "Do you believe this?" He bent his head to kiss her softly, slowly, drugging her more effectively than mulled wine. She closed her eyes and let the honeyed warmth of his intoxication spread through her. When his kiss ended, she felt weak.

"I don't know what to say, Steve." Lauren tried to read his eyes.

"Say you love me." His words poured into her, sweet, soothing, and warming.

"I don't know you that well," she whispered. "But I'd like to."

"Are you warm enough?"

"Yes."

"Good. Let's go find a bear."

"What?" Steve laughed. "You're teasing me."

"Sure I am. You love it, don't you?"

"I'd be lying if I said I didn't."

Resting his chin on her head, he wrapped her in his arms, pulled her back against him, and held her close. "What am I going to do with you?" He exhaled deeply. "How about a walk along the beach? There aren't any stars out yet, but we can pretend." He encircled Lauren's shoulder with a strong arm as they walked in unison.

"You're not homesick, are you?" he asked, breaking the silence. "The sunshine, the beaches, your boyfriend?"

Lauren ignored his pointed question. "I miss it, yes. But I was just wondering about you. You're different. I never know what to expect."

"That's not so bad, is it?"

"No. But I'd like to know more."

Lauren felt Steve tense before he pulled his arm from her shoulder and slid his hands into his pockets. "Not much to tell," he muttered.

Lauren eyed him coldly. "Listen, I don't let anyone kiss me like that, act like it's nothing, then clam up like a total stranger. I don't understand this. Are you afraid of me?"

"Hardly."

"But you're so secretive. Are you afraid to open up?"

"What's the point? I figure when the season is over you'll be on your way to sunny Cal, and that'll be the last of me, right?"

"Well, of course . . . I mean . . . I intend to go back, but—"

"But what?" Two slate-colored eyes bored into her.

"Steve, I know you've been hurt."

"You don't know anything about it. My past is my concern. No one else's." He managed to create an impenetrable wall. Was it to protect his wounded feelings? It was obvious that regardless of the time that had passed since his failed marriage, he still suffered the aftereffects. Before Lauren had a chance to pursue it, the conversation was over.

"Forget it. I'll take you back to the lodge."

A mist rose from the lake, making it appear unfriendly and forbidding. Lauren shivered as her warm feelings dissipated, matching the chilling mood. In stark contrast to the way she had felt earlier, she now looked forward to the shelter that would protect her from the elements.

When they reached the lodge, Lauren escaped to her quarters, unnoticed by Ruth and the lusty group around the table. Closing the heavy door behind her, she insulated herself from the gaiety in the other room.

As though on a speeding, careening roller coaster, Lauren's thoughts rode up and down as she struggled to regain her inner balance. Steve expected her to leave and never come back, just as his wife had left him. But she had to go back. She lived in San Diego. Her business was going to be there. She wanted to be with Steve and Mark, but what could she do? Steve was too guarded, too secretive, uncommunicative. *Is he afraid, or is he hiding something?* It could be that his anger was a facade to protect his secret business dealings, or undisclosed relationships.

She believed she was falling in love. She wanted to. But there was more to love than needs and wants. And for now, her wants came last. She couldn't have him without sacrificing her values, her future . . . her heart. She knew that too. She was exhausted. The vitality she felt before had vanished, as though a candle had been snuffed.

"I saw him leave town. Him and the girl."

"I know. They're in Bethel."

"This makes me nervous."

"You've got enough to take care of without adding worry to it. Just get the job done."

"Listen, you, I've been at this longer than you've been alive. Don't get the notion that you're callin' the shots here."

"I'm not saying that."

"All right, then. I'll call you after it's finished."

"Okay."

Hours had passed when, in her room that was veiled in predawn light, Lauren woke to tapping at the door. A man's voice whispered, "Lauren. Wake up."

Throwing off the covers, she pulled on her robe and opened the door to the tall man who filled the entrance. "Steve! What are you doing here?"

"Shhh." He placed a finger to his lips.

"It's not time to leave, is it?"

"No. It's about two-thirty. Come on. I want to show you something."

"Now?"

"Yeah, come on."

Lauren hastily slipped her shoes on and followed. Outside, he held out his oversize down jacket.

"Here, put this on." He wrapped the front around her like a blanket.

"What is it?"

"You've got to see this. Let's go down by the lake." When they reached the bluff above the beach, Steve pointed to the star-speckled sky.

She could see in the distance the sky shimmering with an eerie curtain of pastel green, white, pink, and yellow, as though an ethereal mantle blew in the soft breeze that surrounded them. "The northern lights," she whispered. "I was so hoping I'd see this."

They stood side by side for several minutes, not touching. Lauren's satiny gown provided little protection from the chilly air that swept around her legs. Enveloped in

Steve's large jacket, she crossed her arms over her chest. Wrapping his long arms around her, he pulled her snugly against him. She leaned back into him as they admired the myriad dancing light forms.

"I'm almost afraid to talk, as if I'd scare it away . . ." she whispered.

He nuzzled her hair, then kissed the hollow below her ear. "That's how *I* feel sometimes . . . almost afraid to say anything that might scare you away."

Turning her to face him, he slipped his arms around her inside the coat and pressed her gently against his chest. They clung to one another in the cool night air. Warmth encompassed her from the tenderness in his voice, and she wondered about this man of conflicts.

"I'm sorry, Lauren. I don't know how to act with you. All I know is . . . I want to be with you," Steve whispered.

"Aren't you forgetting someone?"

"Who? Mark?"

The question that had bothered her all week now demanded an answer. "Sherry. I saw her with you the day I arrived."

Instead of confirming or denying it, he countered, "What about the hotshot you're engaged to? Is he standing in our way?"

His retort startled Lauren.

"This has nothing to do with him or her, Lauren. You and I are here . . ."

Lauren breathed deeply. Her conscience and her ever present concern about Mark propelled her to expose her feelings. "Steve?"

"Mm-hmm."

"I like you. You know that. But I can't go on like this, pretending everything is all right and wondering if you're somehow involved with the sabotage."

Steve's face took on the appearance of that of a practiced poker player—blank, unreadable, and impenetrable.

"My own partner? My own boat?"

"It's been known to happen."

"No."

"Then why hasn't someone been arrested? What will it take? Mark and I could have died."

"You drifted. That was no one's fault."

"But the anchor? The radio?"

Buckner frowned and drew a heavy breath. "I know. I know."

"What about Sherry? Have you had your records audited?"

"No."

"If you'd let me take a look—"

"What good would that do?" he argued. "You're related to my partner. That's as bad as being my partner, don't you see? It wouldn't take a genius to figure out where you spent the past week and tonight—and with whom."

Lauren did see. And she heard. *As bad as being my partner.* To Steve, she was as troublesome as his partner had been. "You've got to get someone to audit your books, Buckner. And you're right, it should be an objective outsider." *One who isn't in love with you.* "You can't deny that there have been rumors and questions—"

"By whom?" he said in a roar. "I've done nothing but good for the fishermen around here. I'm doing my darndest to come up with answers myself."

"Well, I'm concerned about Mark. I'm afraid to go back on the boat not knowing if we'll return, like those brothers."

"You expect me to defend myself against charges you've conjured up in that overworked imagination of yours?"

Lauren winced, steeling herself for the worst. She had done the unthinkable—accused him of murder.

Chapter Seven

The silence that followed was emphasized by the painted sky that had already begun to recede.

"The lights are fading." Steve sighed deeply, and a vague look crossed his features. "Too bad."

Lauren followed his gaze to the pale loveliness that almost blended in color with the morning sky. She sensed that the lights weren't the only things fading.

"I wish it could've lasted longer. I'd like to believe it could." Steve sounded wistful, as though he were speaking about them and not the aurora borealis.

"It doesn't have to end, Steve," Lauren coaxed, her happiness fast becoming a mixture of hurt and confusion. Even after the closeness they had just shared, he was apparently able to overlook it as though it had never happened. It was obvious that he considered their relationship over.

"I did it again." His voice was no longer soft and soothing, but thoughtful and clipped. He shook his head. "Lauren, I think it's best if we don't see each other again." The magic shattered like a broken mirror.

"How do you expect to handle that? My brother is your partner."

"It just won't work, Lauren."

"Steve, if you're innocent—"

"That's a big if. And the fact is, we're worlds apart. You and I don't work."

"You had me figured out from the start, didn't you? Me and my monogrammed luggage."

"You're wrong, Lauren."

"I'm surprised you haven't called me by her name. You gave me every part of her identity but that."

Steve faced her squarely and placed his hands on his fiery opponent's shoulders, as if holding himself safely at arms' distance. "Look, you're very attractive. I find it difficult—impossible—to keep my hands off you."

Her gaze followed his to rest upon her left hand. "I told you before." She clipped her words, trying to maintain a modicum of control. "Richard and I postponed our engagement. We—"

"Then take off his ring."

Lauren gauged the intensity of his face against his angry request. She had not perceived how much this symbol of her link to Richard really affected him. She twisted the ring, and felt it loosen before she pulled it from her finger. "It's my grandmother's." She pulled the ribbon of her gown through the ring and knotted it. "I told you, Richard never bought me anything. I didn't want him to." Lauren's eyes welled with tears. "You're right," she said with finality. "It's best if we don't see each other again. Just get me back to Dillingham so we can forget this night ever happened."

Steve's hands left her shoulders and dropped heavily to his sides. He allowed her to walk away.

The conversation had ended—badly, in Lauren's eyes. But, she had done what she had to do. And if it meant losing a man who couldn't be trusted . . . *Like my grandmother always said. "If you can't trust a man to tell the truth, you can't trust him at all.''* Her limbs felt heavy and encumbered; she couldn't lift the weighted feeling that settled in her chest. She led the way back to the lodge, and hoped no one knew of their tryst under the lights. Lauren had given her heart to this man. She had made her choice, and fate yielded the outcome.

Lauren slept fitfully. Vivid nightmares of the dark-haired pilot wound through her dreams. She felt as if she were constantly reaching for someone, only to lose him in the silent world between waking and sleeping. She was dozing lightly when Ruth called her at 6:00 A.M.

The two had to hurry after breakfast to arrive in Dillingham in time for Mark's call. And under the circumstances, Lauren wanted to leave right away. Steve had barricaded his emotions behind his sunglasses, speaking only when he had to. It seemed evident that Randy also felt something was amiss. Even he seemed subdued and withdrawn.

As they circled above the airstrip, picking up altitude, Lauren searched for the lodge below the tree line and for the spot where they had been not so long before. Steve hid his feelings behind the sunglasses he wore. It seemed to Lauren she had been the only one who had lost at their last meeting—lost her heart and her love.

"Soon as you're through here, Lauren, come on up. Lunch is ready."

"Okay, Emily. Give me five minutes."

"I thought Steven would be in today. . . ." Emily's voice trailed away as she mounted the stairs.

Just for an instant, Lauren wondered if Emily was beginning to question Steve's behavior. *Or is he just avoiding me?* After what had taken place at the lodge, Lauren did not believe he would return until she was gone.

Just the mention of his name weakened her. She struggled with the jumbled emotions she felt. She knew only
that she longed for Steve and regretted the pain of their last
encounter.

When Mark had phoned that morning, he had said that
he needed one more part to fix the propeller. He expected
to have the boat ready to go by the end of next week. For
Lauren, it was none too soon. She hadn't garnered the nerve
to sneak into Steve's office yet, but tonight was the night.
Emily's maid would return after another week, and by then
Lauren would join Mark on the *Ivy*.

Lauren waited until 11:30 P.M., when dusk settled on the
sleepy village. Feeling like a thief, she scanned every bush,
barrel, and shadow for eyes that might be watching. Nervous but determined, Lauren hoped no one would recognize
her.

Weathered wood boardwalks wound through the village
over swampy tundra. She imagined these sidewalks to be
like those depicted in cowboy Westerns, wishing the rich
and hollow sound beneath her tennis shoes were quieter.
Every step seemed to announce her presence.

Lauren spied what looked like tufts of cotton scattered
over the field. She bent to examine them and the other small
flora that grew nearby. Mark had told her about Arctic cotton—a long, green-stemmed plant that looked as if someone had glued a cotton ball on the top. Miniature
wildflowers, like those found on the moisture-laden hills
along the California coast, blossomed in scarlet reds,
whites, and yellows, but their diminutive size made them
almost undetectable. She peered about her in the growing
darkness. If anyone were watching, she hoped they would
assume she was out on a near-midnight nature walk.

Following Mark's directions, Lauren located a two-story
office building that housed various professional services:

the Dillingham Air office; Larry Hoffer, Attorney-at-law; Bristol Bay Fishing Enterprises; and Dennis James, DDS.

A fluorescent orange-and-black sign advertised *Office Space Available—Inquire Within*. Lauren couldn't help but wonder how much office space might cost per square foot here as compared to the expense she expected in La Jolla.

As she slipped into the well-lit, wide corridor, she liked the feel of the building. Exotic potted plants and serigraph pictures complemented the furnishings of the modern complex. The first office, fortunately, was Buckner's. Emblazoned on the window, a royal blue-and gold-swirled logo announced, *Bristol Bay Fishing Enterprises*. She peered between fashionable miniblind slats at an expensively furnished waiting room. *It would take a lot of money to keep a place like this in operation.*

Her heart thumped in her chest. Willing it to cease, she breathed deeply, and cautiously fitted the key in the lock, then slipped inside. She drew the miniblinds closed and clicked on her small 'mag' flashlight.

Mark, I swear, she thought. *The things I do for you. This'll be the last time you talk me into something like this.*

Lauren wiped sweaty palms on her jeans, moved to the front of the desk she presumed to be Sherry's, and then switched on the computer. She eased open a large desk drawer and pointed the beam inside—nail polish, phone book, hand mirror, and cosmetics bag.

She beamed the light around the room for any obvious printouts or ledgers that might contain the information she sought. The computer hummed and beeped, jarring Lauren momentarily. She typed in a directory command, and scanned the contents for an accounting package.

There were several directories that looked interesting, but Lauren pulled up the accounting screen and scrolled through the menus. She found the general ledger and nervously viewed the monitor. It would be hard to determine anything without auditing the entire year's books. She exited the program and switched off the computer.

Behind a closed door, apparently, was Steve's office. Maps of Bristol Bay and tide charts were thumbtacked to the walls. A trash bin sprouted computer printouts and wadded paper.

The desk looked like an administrative disaster area. Papers lay scattered helter-skelter where they fell; invoices amidst mail, magazines, and advertisements. A black-framed retail business license hung on the wall behind an executive chair, proclaiming the business a sole proprietorship owned by Stephen B. Buckner.

A wall clock ticked the seconds, and Lauren listened closely for any other sounds. None. She pointed her light at the file cabinet in the corner; a paperbound printout lay on top.

She lifted the heavy document onto Steve's desk and flipped through the pages. Accounts receivable, payable, financial statements, and general ledgers were arranged chronologically in monthly sequence. It would take weeks of fine-toothing the information to detect discrepancies, if there were any.

She leafed through the folders in the top file drawer and lifted out Mark's file. The remaining file drawers were filled with archive material from previous years.

Anxiously, Lauren tried opening every drawer of the desk. All opened freely, except the bottom one, which was apparently locked.

Lauren opened the middle drawer again and rifled through paraphernalia, looking for loose keys. She wasn't lucky. She did, however, find a small screwdriver. She crouched next to the drawer, flashlight in her mouth this time, trying to aim the beam at the lock.

Laughter from the hallway frightened Lauren into a frozen position. *Keep moving. Keep moving.* She prayed. The outer door opened and closed upon the fading conversation. Whoever it was, they were gone.

Lauren exhaled. *That was close.* Mentally constructing an alibi for herself if she were caught, Lauren continued to work at the stubborn lock. She wedged a ruler into the drawer opening and applied pressure on the screwdriver. It wouldn't budge. She cranked her head underneath the desk to assess the construction. If she worked fast, she might be able to pry the bottom of the drawer out. That idea seemed more feasible than her first, so Lauren unscrewed the fasteners that held the drawer in place and pried off the finishing nails. She checked her watch. She'd already spent eight minutes in the office. Any self-respecting thief should have been in and out in less than half the time, she figured. Her hand slipped and she broke a fingernail. "Darn!" She bit the ripped fingernail and continued prying the drawer.

Lauren leveraged the bottom loose with the metal-edged ruler, and the contents spewed onto the carpet. A small green ledger dropped on top of the sheaf of papers, pens, and assorted business cards beneath his desk.

This might be it. She lifted the book into the muted light and leafed through the pages. It was Steve's personal ledger of transactions between Bristol Bay Fishing and his various contacts—personal boat owners and contractors with whom he evidently conducted business.

The last entry was yesterday's, involving Randy Scott. It appeared to be a payment from Steve based on the Minnow's haul.

Lauren tucked the ledger inside the sleeve of her jacket, slipped Mark's folder against her chest, then zipped her jacket all the way up. She tripped the lock from the inside and pulled the drawer casing out, quickly jammed the bottom back into place, and pressed the nails into the holes. Scooping the contents back into the drawer, Lauren sifted them into place, then slid the drawer into the gaping hole.

Outta here. Lauren returned the screwdriver and ruler, and slipped out of Steve's office. Carefully, she pulled the door closed with an audible click. *Gloves. You should have worn gloves.* Lauren wiped the knob with her sleeve and crossed the reception area to peek through the blinds.

So far, so good. Her heart pounded. *Almost there.* She tried to calm herself. From her vantage point, the hallway looked deserted. She locked the door from the inside, let herself into the hall, and turned the key into the lock to dead-bolt it once again. As she slid the key into her pocket, the front door opened. Lauren jumped back guiltily and gasped.

A pair of icy blue eyes pinpointed their target, and Lauren's knees trembled.

A flash of recognition passed between the two women as the redhead assessed her quarry. ''Mark's little sister . . . Elsie, isn't it?''

''Lauren,'' she corrected.

''I thought Steve—Oh, I see, L. C., for Lauren Cole, right?''

''You're good,'' Lauren replied. ''Sherry, right?''

''What are you doing here? It's a little late to be wandering around, isn't it?''

''I was bored,'' Lauren lied, hoping it didn't show. ''I thought I'd see where the office was.''

''This is it,'' Sherry stated flatly. ''Sometimes I work at night when I can't sleep.''

I'll bet, Lauren thought. Sherry was dressed for a night on the town, and it appeared she'd already been there. *She must enjoy what Dillingham has to offer, including Steve.*

Poised and coiled like a viper ready to strike, Sherry seemed in control of herself. Lauren hoped her quaking knees wouldn't betray her.

''Want to come in?'' Sherry jammed her key into the dead bolt and unlocked it before opening the lower lock.

"Uh, no . . . I don't—"

"You're already here. You might as well see the inside."

Lauren followed Sherry inside, wondering if she suspected anything. She was thankful the room looked undisturbed, since Lauren had replaced everything she had touched.

"Not much to see, is there?"

"It's quite nice." Lauren looked around her as if for the first time.

"That's Steve's office." Sherry tossed her head. "He's gone most of the time, though."

"Too bad."

"What do you mean?"

The hair on Sherry's neck would have stood up had she been a cat. "Nothing. I mean it's too bad he doesn't have a window to look out of. That's all."

Sherry's ire receded noticeably with Lauren's hasty explanation.

"Well . . . ," Lauren moved toward the door. "Thanks, Sherry. I wondered what it looked like in here. Mark has spoken about all of you. . . ." Lauren paused as she realized the blinds on the door remained closed.

Sherry set her purse on her desk and lit a cigarette, exhaling white smoke like a dragon within its lair. "What's your hurry?"

"I thought I'd get back to my room. Gotta get up early and all."

"Thought you were bored? Want to do some of the town?" Sherry suggested.

"No. Thanks anyway. Maybe another time." Lauren's hand gripped the safety of the doorknob.

"Well, let me give you a lift to the hotel. I'm going that way myself." Sherry stubbed the cigarette out in her ashtray and slung her purse strap over her shoulder.

"But weren't you going to do something here? I mean, I don't want to interrupt."

"My pleasure, sugar." Sherry's voice was honey sweet. "My car's outside."

Lauren bit her lip and cursed her misfortune as Sherry led the way to her late-model American sedan. She unlocked her door, which released the passenger's door as well, and Lauren joined her in the plush front seat.

Sherry immediately lit another cigarette and jammed her key into the ignition. The engine roared to life, and she spun out of the gravel parking lot. "So . . . been doing some sight-seeing, have you?"

Feeling as if she were trapped in a snake pit, Lauren tried to quell her discomfort. Wordlessly she looked at Sherry.

"I have eyes. I know where you've been," Sherry went on.

"What are you referring to?"

"You know exactly what I'm referring to. Don't play dumb with me. I'm talking about Steve. You've got it all worked out, haven't you?"

Lauren wasn't sure exactly what Sherry thought she had worked out, but she was sure she didn't like the direction of this conversation.

"Stop the car, Sherry. I'd rather walk."

"Sure you would. Right into Steve's apartment, wouldn't you, sweetie?"

Lauren's anger surfaced and replaced her cool exterior. "Stop the car. Now."

Sherry slammed on the brakes, throwing Lauren forward into the dashboard.

"Watch your step, Lauren," Sherry said in a hiss. "And stay out of my affairs."

Lauren slammed the door after escaping the car, and Sherry sped away, flinging dirt and gravel on her former passenger.

Chapter Eight

By the time she reached her room, Lauren's temper was boiling. She unzipped her jacket, yanked the folder out, and slammed it onto the twin bed, then pulled the ledger from her sleeve, stripped off her jacket, which smelled of Sherry's cigarette smoke, and flung it at the closed door.

Darn Buckner and his whole crew. I'd be happy to stay out of his and Sherry's affairs. Forever.

She flounced onto her bed and flipped the pages of the ledger, fast, then slower. Names of men she'd heard Mark speak of appeared at the top of several pages. Underneath were notes in what she guessed to be Steve's handwriting, detailing loans made to the individuals, and dates. Meager repayments were documented, as well as current balances. This ledger contained personal IOUs that Steve had extended to many of the locals. A quick mental tally showed that Steve had lent out thousands of dollars over the past two years.

The loans puzzled her. She didn't expect to see that. Lauren Frisbeed the book across the room to the adjoining twin bed. ''Nothing,'' she complained to herself and the bare walls. "Nothing. What am I doing here? Any day, Mark. Let's get this show on the road."

"You got the cash?"

"Right here."

Marin counted the bills like a gaming-table pro. " 'Bout time. Don't keep me waitin' so long next time."

"You've got another job to do, don't you?"

"Tonight," Marin groused. "I'll be goin' over this evening."

"Good."

"Have the money ready when I get back. I want to be paid by the job."

"I'll do what I can. It's not easy, you know—"

"What I'm doin' is? Wanna trade places?"

"I'll be waiting when you get back."

The Jeep started up and drove into the darkness without lights until it was well away from the docks.

After work the following Friday, Lauren reached her door and found a note scrawled in her brother's handwriting that read, *Ivy ready—let's go.* A second person had written, *Dinner with me at 8.* It was signed, simply, *Steve.*

Thank goodness. She was happy to learn the boat was ready, but a nagging fear tugged at her subconscious. *Will we be safe?* The second part worried her. *What does Steve want? Did he miss the ledger? Did he find Mark's folder missing?* The worry line between her brows deepened, until she smoothed her fingers over her forehead and cheeks.

She doubted that Sherry would've told Steve about their encounter last week. She wouldn't have the nerve. *I'll just take it as it comes.* Lauren thought. *He's got nothing on me. About as much as I have on him.*

After a long, hot shower, she felt her face relax and her body release the tension she'd built up during the day. She pulled on a cream-colored silk pullover sweater that was not casual, but expensive and feminine. As she smoothed her hand over the soft fabric, her skin tingled with her memory of the feel of Steve's touch. Despite Sherry's claim on him, Lauren felt an exhilaration that she would be seeing Steve tonight.

Precisely at eight, Lauren answered a knock on her door. Until her moist hand slipped off the knob, Lauren hadn't realized how nervous she actually was. She opened the door and met the gray eyes she longed for, yet equally dreaded.

Without speaking, Steve brazenly looked her over as he always did, from head to toe and back again. "Got my note, I see."

Lauren nodded and stepped aside, allowing him to enter her small room. She closed the door, studying him as he looked around, then turned back to face her. She wondered if Sherry experienced the same awful longing she did when Steve was near.

Lauren quivered. She felt like a doe trapped within the confines of her room as he stepped even closer.

"I thought about you all week, Lauren." She backed against the door as Steve spread his hands above her head on both sides of the frame. "You know what it's like being alone, knowing you screwed up—no one to talk to about it?"

Boy, do I ever. Lauren nodded. *According to that ledger, I couldn't have been more wrong about him.*

"I want to apologize for the misunderstanding I caused. Forgive me?"

She felt his breath on her forehead as she gazed into the granite gray eyes. She nodded again, as words would have ruined the effect his closeness had upon her. If he were a pirate, she wanted to be his captive.

"How about dinner? We've got some things to discuss."

"Not fishing, I hope."

Steve laughed. ''I'm sure you excel in many things, Lauren. But I may have a corner on the fishing industry up here.''

''Well, that rules that out. Now I'm intrigued, Mr. Buckner.''

She eased herself out of his arms, then picked up her jacket and purse. ''Shall we go?''

The Inn was a quaint, small-town restaurant. White-washed rock walls and redwood trellises welcomed its guests inside. Steve chose to sit in the patio room, where artificial grapevines hung above them from a redwood gazebo. The lighting was soft and subtle, hidden behind giant leaves of elephant-ear philodendron. The place was nearly deserted on this weekday evening, except for the men who patronized the adjoining bar. Lauren and Steve had the patio all to themselves.

''I was going to try to talk you out of going back with Mark,'' Steve confided, studying her eyes. ''It's dangerous out there. No place for a lady.''

''You mean no place for a California girl like me?''

''I didn't say that,'' he countered. ''But at least in California you're not taking your life in your hands every time you step on board a boat.''

''Are you trying to get rid of me, Buckner?'' Lauren teased, but her question was a two-edged one. It was possible he cared for her and didn't want her risking her life. It was also possible Steve wanted her out of the way so Mark wouldn't be able to make his payment. If that happened, her brother would lose his share of the *Ivy* to Steve.

''Of course not,'' he said soothingly. ''It's just that—''

A smiling waitress brought the liter of cabernet sauvignon that Steve had ordered. He raised his glass in a toast. ''Here's to partners . . .'' Lauren sipped from the long-stemmed glass, her eyes peering over the rim. ''And to their lovely sisters,'' he added.

"To partners," Lauren repeated, raising her glass in salute.

The noise from the bar grew louder, and a man's voice boomed from the other room.

"I don't care—I'm gonna have a little talk. No harm in that."

A heavyset man stumbled out of the other room and encroached upon their intimate setting, a glass in one hand and a bottle in the other.

"Buckner, old friend," he said jeeringly. "How are you doing?" Raising his bottle to his forehead, instead of a hat, he tipped his head to Lauren. "Still raking in the dough, I see."

"You're drunk, Johnson. And I'm entertaining a guest. Talk to me another time, okay?"

Steve's voice carried a defensive, dangerous quality. Lauren's attention was drawn to the obnoxious man who threatened to ruin their evening. The intruder slammed back a gulp of Scotch and sloshed more into the glass from the half-empty bottle he carried. He became more belligerent and aggressive as he spilled a generous amount onto the floor.

"Settle down," Steve warned. "I told you I'd talk with you later."

The large man hunkered down and slid his elbows between the pair, leaning his heavy weight upon his hands.

"I see ya got a new woman here. Did Mallory finally get to you too, or are you still in cahoots with that slime?"

"You're out of line, Johnson," Steve stated with deadly calm. "Move along."

Barely able to maintain his balance, Johnson faced the girl. His head bobbed back and forth, and his breath smelled strongly of Scotch. His bloodshot eyes tried to focus on Lauren, as if he knew who she was. "You Cole's sister?"

Lauren nodded numbly, wishing he'd go away.

"I just wanna know one thing, li'l lady . . . is he giving you what he's giving your brother?" he said with a sneer. "A good—"

Before Johnson could finish what he tried to say, Steve yanked him backward. The large man crashed into an empty table and chairs, then slid down onto the floor.

The glass of Scotch he'd carried splattered over Lauren's sweater before it fell and broke. The bottle flew in another direction and spun crazily before rolling to a stop against the far wall. The commotion compounded as several people ran from the lounge area and converged onto the patio.

"Monsieur Buckner!" The owner, Jean-Pierre, hurried from the kitchen, wiping his hands on the white baker's apron that was tied around his globular middle. "What is this? Shall I call the police?"

Steve faced the man's drinking buddies and said in a roar, "Get this lowlife out of here before I really lose my temper."

Lauren felt her face drain of color. She dabbed the stiff linen napkin on her wet sweater, feeling soiled and humiliated.

"Are you all right, monsieur? Mademoiselle?" Jean-Pierre fretted over his ruffled guests and pranced around them nervously. "*Mon Dieu,* what a night."

Muttering and grumbling, four men dragged Johnson outside, knocking chairs aside as they went.

"I'm sorry, Lauren," Steve muttered.

"What was that all about?" she asked when her speeding heart slowed.

"A disgruntled former associate, that's all."

"Who doesn't like Mallory, I take it." Lauren could see Steve was still agitated, as he gripped his balled hand. *This could be what I've been afraid of. Perhaps, finally, I'm going to learn the truth—good or bad—about him. Oh, Steve, don't let it be true,* she prayed.

"Is it possible there's some discrepancy—"

Steve glowered at her.

"Has Sherry—"

"Leave her out of this," Steve snapped. "It's not your problem."

"If it affects Mark, it is my problem," Lauren argued. "It seems Johnson is holding quite a grudge." *And, apparently, so are you, Mr. Buckner.* As much as she wanted to know about Steve's business dealings, she dreaded the truth if it meant she and her brother had been taken in by a swindler. "How many others—"

"My affairs are my business. Not yours. Not his," Steve shouted. "Why is it I'm the bad guy no matter what I do? I can't even enjoy a simple meal." Steve's retort evoked more stares from the few who remained on the patio.

His harsh words embarrassed her, and Lauren felt she was seeing the ruthless side of Steve that he'd managed to hide until now. Tears pricked her eyes, and she futilely tried wiping them with the nonabsorbent linen.

He slammed his fist on the table, rattling silverware and crystal, and swore.

Lauren stood abruptly and threw her napkin down.

"Lauren, wait." Steve grabbed her arm, but she jerked free. "Let me drive you home."

"Why? So you can treat me the way you treat Mark? No, thanks." She marched to the foyer, yanked her jacket from the closet, and left the coat hanger clanging back and forth on the metal rod.

Tears spilling over her face made seeing difficult as she stormed back toward the hotel. The buildings loomed darkly around her, and the fog she had grown to love now felt icy and cold as the droplets formed on her cheeks and chin. The wind she created by her fast pace roared in her ears and caused her to walk faster, as if the devil were after her.

When she reached the safety of her room, Lauren threw

herself facedown on the single bed and sobbed as though her heart had been wrenched from her.

Lauren's thoughts rolled and swelled like the churning tides. Nothing made sense. Buckner's actions seemed incongruous with his treatment of her. If he was the saint Mark made him out to be, it didn't show. Her heart felt one thing, but her eyes saw another, and her logic was nonexistent. It took some time to harness her runaway emotions, but when she did, Lauren's will was as unbending as a steel rod. She gathered her things and left the hotel. She was going to meet Mark at Naknek.

A native outside the trading post had given her the name of a fisherman who might take her to the Naknek Cannery, where Mark waited. It had been easy enough to find Harvey Marin. He was the only boatman in the harbor.

"Mr. Marin?" Lauren addressed the back of the man rummaging in his cabin. When he turned around, she avoided looking at him directly, wishing to conceal her tear-swollen eyes.

"Yeah. What d'ya want?"

"I hear you take passengers. I need to go to Naknek."

"When?"

"Now. Right away."

She felt the man's gaze upon her and heard a sound like the scratch of stubble on an unshaven chin.

"Lucky for you I was goin' over anyway. Give me a few minutes. I'll be ready and you can board."

She checked her watch. It was almost 9:30 in the evening, but the light looked more like late afternoon. While she waited on the dock, her thoughts wandered back to the man she had walked out on earlier. She should have known better than to fall in love. Even worse, with Mark's partner.

Sitting forlornly on her duffel bag, Lauren gazed at the filthy harbor that was littered with empty liquor bottles, pieces of floating trash, and oil slicks that dotted the water in lazy rainbow swirls. It disgusted her.

"Get your gear on board," the rough-looking man barked. "Let's go."

Lauren muscled the heavy bag from the weathered wood dock onto the deck of the moored craft. She accepted the hand Marin offered to steady her as she stepped aboard. Only then did she briefly allow their eyes to meet. She stifled a gasp when she recognized the brooding, hateful eyes of the derelict she had seen outside the tavern days before. His angry gaze frightened her now as much as it had the day she and Steve had flown to Bethel.

"It'll cost you twenty-five. Still wanna go?"

"Yes ... of course ..." Lauren stammered. She dropped her gaze to her wallet, warding off his unwelcome inspection of her, and pulled out a crisply folded twenty and a five-dollar bill. Maybe she had only imagined his character flaws, she quickly rationalized. As she handed him the money, she said, "I'm going to meet Mark Cole. My brother."

"Oh, yeah?" he said, stroking his stubbled chin, smiling lazily. "I know Mark. Heard you were in town."

The smile lingered too long for Lauren's comfort. She hoped she hadn't run from trouble only to find more.

"Sit down in there." He directed her toward a dark cabin. "We'll get under way."

Lauren's breath escaped her like air from a deflating balloon. She brushed past the older man, hoping he would dismiss her without further conversation. As they plowed through the inky water, Lauren, preoccupied with the earlier events of the evening, chose to ignore the leering glances he stole.

Lauren picked out the *Ivy* among several boats that lined the cannery dock, moored in the same spot where she had seen the boat three weeks ago. The little boat bobbed in the water, looking ready to be put to sea again.

Chapter Nine

‘‘There's Mark.’’ Anxious to put distance between her and Marin, Lauren grabbed her bag and hurried from the strong-smelling cabin to leave the fisherman's vessel. ‘‘Appreciate it, Mr. Marin.’’

‘‘Anytime. You come see Harvey again, anytime.’’

Mark leaped onto the dock and sprinted across the wooden planks toward his sister.

‘‘Lauren,’’ he bellowed, and squeezed her against him in a giant bear hug. ‘‘You're looking good. Taking care of yourself, I see.’’ A mischievous smile lit his face.

‘‘I've been fine. Glad to get your note.’’

‘‘How about Steve. Did you see him?’’ Lauren turned her head. ‘‘What's the matter? You two have a fight or something?’’

Even though the feelings she had once felt for Steve seemed forever lost, Lauren had not believed the depth of her emotional involvement. She had given her heart to a man whom she thought would return her love, but he apparently had no regard for her or the other people he used.

On Marin's boat, she had fought with herself for over an hour, wondering if she should tell Mark what had taken

135

place at the restaurant. Finally faced with the decision, she opted to wait until morning. It was still too fresh, too painful. The ledger had proved useless, and until she had tangible evidence against Steve, she knew Mark wouldn't accept it.

"I think I'll go below and make coffee. I brought some groceries. How does beef stew sound for dinner tomorrow?"

"Great. I knew there was a reason I missed you." Mark laughed. "Nice to have you aboard, mate."

Mark estimated that their downtime had cost them several thousand dollars. Over breakfast, Lauren told Mark about Johnson and the incident at the restaurant. She produced the file folder and Steve's ledger, allowing Mark to leaf through them.

"I told you . . . it's not Steve," Mark said quietly.

"But what about Johnson? He seemed convinced he'd been cheated. And you too, for that matter."

"I don't know about him. All I know is that Steve wouldn't deliberately cheat anyone."

"There's something else I wanted to tell you, Mark. The night I left the office, I had a run-in with Sherry."

"Oh, yeah? What'd she have to say?"

"She seemed to think I was—"

"Hello." A knock and heavy steps interrupted. "Anybody home?"

"Yeah, Steve. Down here."

Lauren's heart raced. "Steve? Oh, no, Mark."

"Got room for one more?" Steve asked.

"It's about time you showed up. I thought we'd have to shove off without you." Mark accepted the gear Steve handed him.

"You knew he was coming? Mark, you should have told me."

"Sit down, Lauren, and cool your jets," Mark ordered. "Come on in, Steve. Coffee's hot."

Lauren slipped the ledger and folder under the cushion before Steve descended into the room. Feeling embarrassed, guilty, and angry at the same time, she stared at Mark, tight-lipped.

"Lauren," Steve said as he scooted onto the bench seat.

"If I'd known you were coming," Lauren muttered, "*I* wouldn't have."

"Now wait a minute, Lauren. Steve's here to help out and ensure we don't meet with any more accidents. Surely you don't object to that?"

"Mark, if you didn't need me, I wouldn't be here. There's no point in both of us staying."

"There is," Mark insisted. "Talk to her, Steve. I'll be right back."

"Lauren," Steve began; "I want to apologize."

"For what?"

"Last night. This morning. You name it."

"Don't bother."

"I will anyway. I'm sorry. I shouldn't have lost my temper." He looked at her as if seeking her forgiveness. "I didn't mean to upset you."

"But you did." Lauren looked at him through teary eyes. "I don't know what to believe, Steve. I'm confused and I don't like feeling this way."

"I am too. It seems like everything I've tried to do is blowing up in my face. I don't know what's going to hit me next. But I promise not to make it harder on you. Will you forgive me?" he asked, stretching his hand across the table to her.

Lauren acknowledged his apology with a nod as she fought to hold back her tears.

"I'm sorry too," she said simply. She rose from her seat and began gathering her belongings.

"Okay, I'm back." Mark bounded into the nook. "What'd I miss? Wait a minute. Where are you going, Lauren?"

"I'm through here. You don't need me."

"What are you talking about? Of course we need you, don't we, Steve?"

"Darn right," Steve agreed. "I'm not about to cook for someone who prefers to eat out of tin cans. Lauren at least has an appreciation for civilized meals."

"Besides," Mark interjected, "we need someone to help man the helm, navigate the swells, beat us at cards, complain about our dirty clothes, stuff like that."

Lauren laughed in spite of her runaway emotions.

Steve cupped his hands around Lauren's. "Stay with us, Lauren. Please."

Having Steve on board gave Lauren an opportunity to witness hard work in action. Steve and Mark worked side by side gaffing salmon from the nets. She enjoyed their verbal sparring and camaraderie. It felt good to listen to grown men laugh and joke like kids. Steve's presence created an atmosphere of security and safety, as if nothing could harm them while he was there.

"There's Randy's Minnow." Mark pointed out a sleek-looking, silver-and-red-striped boat that motored south about three hundred fathoms away from them.

"Wow." Lauren blocked the light with her hand and stared at the sleek vessel. "It looks brand-new."

"It is," said Steve. "He's spent a lot of money on that boat."

"Worked hard for it too," Mark stated.

"Looks like he's heading out again." Lauren watched as the powerful boat pulled into the distance.

"Miller's subleasing it, and they're splitting the haul. He's got a crew of natives hired on."

"So do I," Mark crowed. "Come on, swabs. Back to work."

The three of them worked hard to make up their misfortune. By the end of the week they had their hold filled with king salmon. Over the course of days, Lauren made friends with Steve on a less intimate level. She came to trust him as Mark seemed to, and the three shared a private world isolated by wind and sea.

She had experienced several sides of this man; he was sensitive, thoughtful, capable, calculating, and tender—all of which endeared him to her further. She particularly enjoyed watching Mark and Steve together. The serious, forceful Steve teaming with frivolous, good-natured Mark provided a workable balance, it seemed.

When it was time to unload their catch, Steve radioed the *Arctic Queen* and waited for the floating scow to come alongside. Standing on the bow with the mooring rope in hand, Lauren waved at the *Queen*'s crew as it pulled alongside within throwing range. The *Arctic Queen*'s crew chief, a short, stocky Aleut Indian named Oscar, took a liking to Lauren. Affectionately, she named him King Oscar, because he supervised his crew like a monarch preparing for battle.

"Get that hook ready, Oscar," Lauren shouted. "We've got at least five tons today."

"Lucky fish," he called back. "To be caught by such a woman. Halloo, Mark. Halloo, Steve." He waved at them and flashed a broken-toothed grin.

When he addressed his men, he became king, lord of the scow. Barking orders like an imperial tyrant, he strutted back and forth along the bridge; a gaff hook as his scepter, he used it to point with and to direct his men.

The hands all turned-to and scurried to carry out his commands. They brought the catch into the saltwater hold and got the boat under way to the other fishing vessels, before making a run to the cannery.

Lauren unhooked the brailer line and attached each loop onto the giant hook as Mark had taught her. She had mastered the task and now thought nothing of the demanding work. What at first had been awkward and frustrating—using what she termed muscle, not matter—she now accomplished with dexterity and skill. She tried unsuccessfully to keep Steve's warmth and tender kisses off her mind while she worked, by mentally calculating how many more fish it would take to pay Mark's share of the boat.

The men vacated the cabin after breakfast to allow Lauren time to freshen up with "spit baths." Her perfume helped to mask the moldy smell of the cabin to an extent, but by the end of the day she didn't care. She welcomed her bed, smell or no smell.

Steve and Mark bunked above and below on the port side, while Lauren kept her bunk on the starboard side. Mark fashioned a curtain with fishing hooks and line that established some privacy for her within this community sleeping arrangement.

She succumbed to sleep nightly with pleasant dreams of the dark-haired man holding her until she dozed. But Steve, if he had any feelings for her, disguised them and kept his distance. It seemed he had withdrawn from her completely, and, except for occasional friendly glances, he avoided any contact while on board the *Ivy*. It was a relief to Lauren when he announced at the end of the two-week period that he would leave at Naknek when they docked.

She missed Steve after he'd gone. He left an emptiness in her heart, and the days stretched interminably. After mid-July, the fishing slowed. They caught a few hundred kings, but most stopped running after the July Fourth weekend. The reds were gone, and silvers seemed harder to come by.

Silver schools weren't as large as the red schools, and they seemed more elusive as the season waned. They now waited for the chum—the salmon that ran once every four years. Fortunately, this was a good year for chum.

During the closed-season periods, Lauren read and slept while Mark filled his time whittling small animal figures from driftwood burls and whistling along with the radio.

Lauren knew it would soon be time for her to leave. She regretted the time she had wasted suspecting Steve, then ignoring him when he was around her. But she knew their worlds collided, not complemented, and there would be no fixing that.

Finally their four-week fishing stint ended, and a post-season celebration ensued. Mark bounded out of the cabin wearing wrinkled, baggy gray trousers, a short-sleeved T-shirt, and a pink knit tie. He balanced his boom box on his shoulder with one hand and snapped his fingers in time to a heavy-metal beat.

"Come on, Lauren," he urged. "Get with it." He grabbed her hand, spun her around, and gyrated his hips in an exaggerated Elvis imitation.

"No, thanks." She laughed. "I think I'd rather beat the rest of you crazed fishermen into town." Lauren pulled her T-shirts down from the clothesline they'd strung from the bow to the bridge and pranced below. "I can't wait for a real shower."

"Aw, c'mon," Mark coaxed. "I've got to stay to pick up our check tomorrow, and I can't miss a party. That gives us two reasons to stay."

"If I can find a ride in, I'm leaving tonight while the tide is high."

"All right. If that's what you want. Just be careful."

"Of course." Lauren kissed her brother on the cheek. "I'll be waiting for you when you get in. Just radio ahead."

His loud music faded as Lauren stepped from the *Ivy*

onto the crowded dock. She scanned the boats that remained, hoping to see someone on board who might be preparing to leave for Dillingham. Craning her head, she took another look around, then caught sight of Harvey Marin's boat.

"Mr. Marin? Are you there? Mr. Marin?"

"Looking for someone?" said a voice behind her.

Lauren twisted around and barely avoided bumping into him. "Oh—you surprised me." She gasped.

"What d'ya need?"

"I need a ride to Dillingham. Are you going there tonight?"

"I might . . . I was just beginnin' to enjoy myself, though." He nodded toward the boisterous crowd. "What did you have in mind?"

"Well, you charged me twenty-five dollars before. I could pay extra . . . maybe thirty-five?"

A low chuckle escaped the graveled throat. "Sure. We don't need all these noisy people botherin' us anyway, do we now?"

The smile left her face, and she felt as if she had just struck a bargain with the devil. "I'll get my things and be right back." Lauren sprinted back toward her brother and shouted over his music, "Harvey Marin's taking me in. See you tomorrow."

Mark nodded, keeping time with the music.

A niggling doubt raised itself as Lauren gathered her things, but she dismissed it as the product of her overcautious nature. Ignoring it, she jammed the last of her clothes into the duffel bag and zipped it closed.

"I'm ready, Mr. Marin." Lauren swung her bag on board and scrambled over the side.

"Name's Harvey," he said in a slur.

"Okay, Harvey."

"Throw that line off, will you?"

Lauren untied the mooring line and wound it on the bow as Harvey idled the boat away from the others. She had become accustomed to the sound of powerful gurgling diesel engines, and the noise prompted a feeling of control over the intimidating presence of the ocean.

As they reached the mouth of Naknek Inlet, instead of giving it full throttle, Harvey cut the engine, then swaggered to the bow and threw the anchor overboard.

"What's the matter, Harvey?" Lauren asked, her fear moving toward panic. The wicked dark eyes she had avoided before now arrested hers.

"I thought we'd settle the bill before we got to town." A thick tongue parted and moistened his lips before he wiped them with the back of a grimy hand.

"Oh, sure . . ." Lauren edged away and reached into her duffel bag for her wallet. Cold, stubby fingers gripped her forearm, paralyzing her with fear. She looked up into the face that was now cloaked in an evil smile.

"I have to get my money." Lauren's voice trembled, but she tried to appear confident and unafraid.

"That's not all I want," he said with a growl like a cur itching for a fight. Tightening the grip on her arm, he forced her to face him.

"No." She jerked loose and backed away. "I'll pay you what you want. That's all." Lauren's heart beat wildly against her ribs.

Fury evident in the man's eyes, he spat out, "You women are all alike. You tease a man to get what you want; then you back off. . . ." He wiped his mouth with his sleeve.

"No." She screamed, "Mark!"

"He can't hear you. Not now. Kinda like when you lost your radio, isn't it?"

His words increased her terror as she realized she was dealing with a criminal.

"Listen, Harvey . . . take me back to the cannery."

"Think you're too good for ol' Harvey—is that it?"

Lauren tried to escape the confining cabin, but he blocked the exit and shoved her back. She felt a bruise rising where her thigh slammed against the table. The shock of pain made her realize she was no match against his physical strength. She had to outwit him.

"I'll pay you double, Marin."

"You don't have to put on an act. I've seen you come and go with Buckner. You ain't no angel." Crushing her against the filthy bunk, Marin scraped his stubbled face against her smooth skin.

At that moment, the sound of an outboard motor cut into the cabin. "Lauren, are you there?"

Harvey cursed the intrusion and backed away as she broke free. A shadow blanketed the doorway, and Lauren charged headlong into Steve Buckner.

Chapter Ten

"What's going on here, Marin?" Steve's low tone crackled with menace. Lauren bolted past him into her brother's arms, while Steve faced the disheveled boatman.

"That's obvious, isn't it? The little lady was tryin' to pay her transportation—that's all."

"That's a lie!" Lauren raged. "He tried to . . . he wanted to . . ." Lauren struggled to free herself from her brother's grip and confront her enemy, but Mark restrained her.

"Come out of there, Marin," Steve demanded, "before I drag you out."

Lauren watched as Steve's muscular arms rippled with his suppressed rage, and his fists balled at his side.

"Now just a minute, Buckner. You're on *my* boat."

Mark pushed himself between his friend and Lauren's assailant. "Lauren's okay, Steve. Let's get her out of here."

"You were too darned good to take my boat before. You're trespassing, Buckner," Marin threatened.

"Is that why you've been crippling my boats? Trying to get even?"

"What's the matter? Can't stand a little healthy competition. mate? Free enterprise—isn't that what you call it?''

Steve's jaw twitched angrily, and he struggled to control his clenchéd fists. ''What *I* call it is destruction of personal property, assault and battery, and, if we can prove it, murder. You're looking at a lot of time, Marin.''

The seaman's face paled. ''Now hold on, Buckner, you ain't gonna pin no—''

''Tell me about it, Marin. How did those boys die out there? Was that part of your plan?''

Marin's jaw slackened as he struggled to form his words. ''You've got no proof. How're ya gonna—''

''Sherry told me all about it.'' Silence pervaded.

Lauren wondered if Marin was guilty or if Steve was merely calling his bluff. What had Sherry confessed? It didn't seem to matter. Marin had taken the bait.

''It was their idea—the two of 'em. They promised to fix me up when your company floundered. Never could trust them bleedin' kids. Wait till I get hold of Randy.''

Steve faltered for a moment, as though the man's words were news to him, but instantly regained his composure.

''You're going to issue a statement, Marin. I'm not through with you.''

''But—''

''Save it for the cops,'' Buckner continued, ''and you'll help us prove it, or you'll hang alone.''

The Fish and Game cutter pulled alongside with the police on board. Marin was cuffed and taken aboard the cutter, while his boat was piloted back to Naknek by a game warden.

''Get in the boat, Lauren,'' Mark ordered quietly. ''I'll get your things.''

Lauren had heard enough. She allowed Mark to help her into the smaller craft. Still angry and in a mild state of shock, she sat rigidly on the bench of the borrowed outboard and stared straight ahead, while Steve piloted them back toward the cannery.

"He knew about th-the radio, M-Mark," Lauren stuttered as adrenaline surged in her system.

"I know." Mark circled his arms about his sister. "Steve came with the police to arrest Marin when they found out he'd taken off. I told Steve you were with him. Are you all right? Did he hurt you."

She rubbed the welt she felt rising on her thigh, easing the pressure of the bruise, and shook her head. "Just my pride. Thanks, Mark. I'm glad you showed up when you did."

"I had a feeling about that guy, Lauren. I tried to ignore it and let you go, but it was like, you know, like the time you got sick at camp and I made Mom drive me there to check on you."

"I know. It's always been that way with us. That's why I came to Alaska. I thought my being with you would somehow help keep you safe. Didn't seem to work for me, though."

Mark pulled his sister closer.

"How could I have been so stupid?" She shuddered, thinking how it might have turned out had her brother and Steve not been there to intervene. "Thank you, Mark."

"Thank Steve. He landed about the same time you left. He spotted Marin's boat," Mark added. "When we saw it anchored we thought you might be in trouble. We got here as quickly as we could. I'm sorry, Lauren. I should have taken you in myself."

She shook her head.

"Steve's going to fly you back. Just sit tight till I get there. And listen"—he raised her chin with his finger—"don't take up with any more sailors, OK?"

Mark's teasing broke the emotional tension, and in spite of herself, Lauren laughed.

*   *   *

Steve's dark brows drew together in a frown, marring his otherwise handsome face. Lauren could not tell if the anger was directed at her or at the people he had once considered his friends. Although they were separated by mere inches, they could have been miles apart. She edged closer to her side of the plane and stared out the window. Thick stands of birch, interspersed with spruce, towered over small ponds that dotted idyllic tundra meadows. Soaring high above the earth had a calming effect on her until she saw the miniature-scale buildings and vehicles of Dillingham appear in the distance.

The muscles in Lauren's neck constricted and ached. She became aware of a throbbing headache until she shed the tears she had previously held captive. Her wind-chapped face burned where scalding tears streamed, unchecked.

"I'm sorry you had to go through that." Lauren jumped when Steve gently touched her arm. "You were right about Sherry, you know. She tampered with my accounts from the start."

"How'd you get her to admit it? Did you have your books audited?"

"I spent the last two weeks back and forth with an IRS investigating team in Anchorage checking my records and her background. She's made the rounds."

"What about Randy? Did she say—"

Steve shook his head and exhaled as if it pained him. "I still can't believe it. I've known him for years. I'm sure she put him up to it."

"I thought she was after you. I had no idea—"

"I guess she gave up and wanted revenge. She undermined my entire operation. Nearly succeeded too."

"She never gave up," Lauren stated. "But I can't believe she wanted you to suffer. Incredible."

"The sad thing is that she apparently strung Randy along. Poor kid didn't have a chance."

"What's going to happen to him . . . to all of them?"

"Sherry's in custody now, Marin's going to be taken in and questioned. I suppose Randy will be arrested too. I don't know. I'm sure it's his first encounter with the law. I couldn't say the same about Marin and Sherry."

"And her father?"

"Don't know. Seems he's always following Sherry around, picking up the pieces. I don't know what he'll do." Steve squeezed her hand. "I want to thank you for helping bring this into the open. Who knows how long it would have continued?"

She wanted to accept his healing words and lean against him. She wanted to take back the whole summer and start again. "I was so wrong about you, Steve."

"I'm glad you were. If not for you, I wouldn't have been so driven to prove my innocence and find out what was really going on." Lauren sobbed. He had seen women cry before, but he had hardened himself against it, until now. His stomach tightened into a cold ball, and his helpless feeling took the form of quiet resolve—nothing would ever harm her again, if he had any say about it. He studied Lauren. In stark contrast to the dark-haired natives and sourdoughs he encountered daily, her golden-blond hair radiated red-gold from the filtered sunlight. Cloudy skies had softened her California tan to an attractive creamy beige tone.

When he gently pried her fingers from her face, he felt the newly acquired calluses that had formed on her palm. Wordlessly, he wiped at a tear that had begun its descent over her cheek.

His gentleness made her feel even more vulnerable and weak. "I'm so humiliated. I don't know why I ever came."

"Pretty hard on yourself, aren't you?"

"I used to think I was in control of myself and my life, but since I came here, it seems I'm wrong about everything."

"You handled yourself pretty well under the circumstances, Lauren."

She looked outside to determine their location, and discovered they had long since flown over Dillingham. He must have read the question on her face.

"I thought you could stand a little R and R. What do you think? There's this little cabin I know of."

Lauren leaned her throbbing head back and closed her eyes, remembering the last trip she had taken with Steve—the fire of their kisses, the ice of their departure.

"I'll bring Mark up Sunday and we can all fly back together Monday morning. How does that sound? I'll give you all the space you need, Lauren." His words poured over her in soothing waves. "That is, if you want my company. I could just drop you off and leave you there alone."

"I don't have a gun," she blurted. "What about the bears?"

"There's a shotgun beneath the sink, but I won't tell you where I keep the shells until I leave. You may decide to use it on me before the weekend is over."

"I promise, Steve. I'm sticking to what I know: cooking, eating, reading, and accounting."

"Well, it wouldn't hurt you to relax a little. You haven't had an easy time of it."

Lauren closed her eyes, drew in a deep breath, and wished they were already there. Steve brought the pontoon plane down into the bay. A mild jolt and gushing spray told her they had landed safely. When they neared the dock, the engines were cut. Water slapped against the plane and gently bounced it on its fluid bed as they drifted the last few yards toward the tie-down. The comforting sound filled

Lauren with a pleasantness as she was rocked with each wave.

"Here we are. Are you all right?"

"I'll be okay," Lauren replied. His kindness disarmed her. She surveyed the cabin silently and decided it was even prettier than she had remembered. A recent rain scented the air with the sharp smell of spruce and moist, clean earth. The crystal lake sparkled with sunshine that seemed to flash on and off like a light between passing clouds. She could see the bottom of the cove as though looking through a glass-bottomed boat.

"Let's unload our gear. I'll get a fire going." Steve bounded from the plane, while Lauren, feeling drained from her narrow escape, followed behind, moving slower than normal.

Steve carried Lauren's duffel bag inside and set it beside the large bed. "You can sleep there, Lauren. I'll take the bunk."

"No. I'll take the bunk. I'm smaller than you."

"You're right," he agreed. "I just wanted you to be comfortable."

"The bunk suits me fine."

"Ok. Now, let's see . . . what shall we have for dinner? Canned hash, stew, ravioli, peaches?"

"I'm not very hungry right now. Is there something I could use to wash in?"

"Sure. I'll get some water from the lake. You can use this." Steve pulled a large aluminum pot from beneath the counter and set it atop the propane stove. After he returned with water, Steve set aside a towel, a washcloth, and one of his oversize T-shirts for her.

"What's this?" She held the shirt to her chest and it draped below her knees.

"A nightgown." He grinned. "It doesn't smell like salmon slime and mildew. I'm going out to chop wood so we can keep old Ironsides full this weekend. If you need anything, I'll be right here.''

She appreciated the privacy he allowed her without making it seem awkward or obvious. When the water reached a boil, Lauren added cold water to it, and brought it down to a moderate temperature. She stripped off her clothing and vigorously scrubbed the telltale scent of the boats from herself. More water was boiled to shampoo her hair. When she was through, Lauren felt clean and purged.

She pulled on her jeans and Steve's oversize T-shirt, then dragged a large-toothed comb through her hair. The sound of Steve chopping wood ceased, and Lauren opened the door.

As late evening approached, the sky's color had transformed from a pale blue infinity to a majestic silver background streaked with long pink slashes of clouds.

''It's okay to come in,'' Lauren called.

''Good,'' Steve said, as he carried an armload of wood inside. ''I hope you're hungry, because I'm starved.''

Lauren took on the task of kitchen duty, deciding which cans of food to prepare, then choosing the necessary pots. Her eyes repeatedly strayed to Steve's tall figure, reassuring her he was with her, as he carried wood from outside and stacked it against the wall. ''The wood smells good, Steve.'' She sighed dreamily. ''I'll always remember the way you smell of spruce, and why.''

He answered her with a smile, then stood back and assessed the neat pile of logs. ''There. That should give us enough heat for a while,'' he said, wiping his hands noisily against each other.

''Dinner's on,'' Lauren announced.

''What? No candlelight, no musicians? Where's the linen tablecloth?'' Steve feigned dismay.

It was obvious to Lauren he was trying extra hard to lift her spirits and pull her out of the depression she was feeling. Lauren looked over the smooth-topped table she'd set, with one camp fork at each aluminum plate, chipped enameled mugs, and the separate bowls of canned hash and peaches.

"Any sourdough can see we're roughin' it, mister. Take it or leave it."

Grabbing her around the waist, Steve pulled Lauren against his hard, lean body and said with a growl, "How about we forget dinner for a while?"

She fought his grasp instinctively, reacting to her too-recent confrontation with Marin. Steve quickly released her.

"I'm sorry, Lauren. I shouldn't have done that."

"No," she said quietly. "Don't let me go. Hold me. Please."

Gently, he took her in his arms and held her. She buried her face in his shirt and felt the strong, steady staccato beating of his heart. Molding herself to him, she allowed her weight to rest heavily against his strong frame.

She thought back to the last time they had been together like this. The evening had been disastrous, and she had left him, convinced he was cheating her brother. She raised her lashes and peered into his face. Looking at him now through love-softened eyes, she saw the pirate who pillaged her dreams. They stood for several minutes until she became aware of the steady increase of his heartbeat. His nearness disturbed her ability to think clearly, and when she raised her face to his, she felt her strength dissolve under his gray gaze.

"I missed you, Steve."

"I missed you," he said, his voice rich and heavy.

"Dinner's on," she repeated.

"Forget dinner." His lips reverently took possession of hers.

She fantasized that she and Steve were again on the great

lawn at the North Star Lodge beneath the northern lights. He lovingly caressed her face and fingered a misplaced curl. She smelled spruce on his hands, mixed with the scent from his soft woolen shirt. In his protective arms, she felt as if his sweet, warm smell wrapped around her and branded her as his alone. Lauren focused on the face of the man she loved. The man she would always love.

"Steve?"

"Yes?"

"Thank you."

"For what?" he asked, looking surprised.

"For bringing me here."

He combed his fingers through her hair. "I guess we should eat before it gets cold."

"Good idea."

After dinner, Steve lay on top of the love-apples quilt and soon fell asleep. Lauren pulled a quilt from the bunk and drew it over his sleeping form. She watched him as he slept, and saw the boy, the man, gentle and calm—removed from the pressures of work and manhood, transported into the blissful realm of life-renewing sleep. One arm lay curled above his head, the other across his chest.

When the fire in Ironsides smoldered to red embers, she crawled into her own bunk and succumbed to her own sweet dreams.

Lauren's eyelids fluttered. The sound of someone stirring near the propane stove interrupted her slumber before she fully realized where she was. She turned sleepy eyes to see Steve dressed in jeans and a woolen shirt, busily preparing a pot of coffee. The burner was turned on high, and the small table was decorated with a blueberry sprig. The sweet smell of muffins on the range beckoned Lauren. At ease with the demands of flying a plane, running a business, piloting a boat or making breakfast, Steve was amazing.

"You're awake. . . ." His voice cascaded rich and deep around her ears.

"Ummm . . ." she murmured contentedly.

"Not quite awake."

"Uh-huh . . ."

Lauren imagined him as a pirate, home from his high-seas adventures, silk shirt partially buttoned, her fingers playing in the soft field of hair on his manly chest, circling the contours. She lay back on the bed, pulling the quilt up to her chin. She watched as he moved from the front of the stove to her side—his long frame a study in grace of motion. Two strides closed the small space between them; then he sat beside her on the bunk.

"I was just making coffee and muffins. Do you want some?"

"Yes. Thank you."

He tugged at a springy curl. "Thank you."

"For what?" she asked, surprised.

"For coming here."

Feeling pampered and unhurried, Lauren stretched like a waking feline, then lay there, content to watch. "You'll have to teach me how to make those muffins, so when I get lonesome for Alaska I can fix them."

"Put your swimsuit on. We'll go kayaking in a while."

"You'll have to leave the room then. I can't change with you in here."

After he stepped outside, Lauren threw off the quilt, slipped her swimsuit and jeans on, then sprinted outside to the water's edge. Kneeling, she cupped ice-cold water in her hands and splashed her face. Fully awake now, she was hungry and ready to eat when she reentered the cabin.

After breakfast, Lauren and Steve launched the kayak and paddled the peaceful lake. After a couple of hours, they beached the craft and strolled along the shore. With his arm draped comfortably over her shoulders, he pointed out tracks of bear and moose. Lauren grew pensive as she listened to him. She wanted to tell him she loved him, but dared not.

"Race you back, Lauren."

"Oh, yeah? Want to place bets?"

"Why not? I put all my money on me."

"Why, you conceited—"

"Now, now. Name-calling won't help you. Didn't your mother ever tell you—"

"Go!" Lauren shouted.

Lauren sprang ahead, stretching her legs ahead of her with all the strength she could muster. Cool air burned her lungs as she forced her breath in and out. Steve struggled to overtake her; then they ran abreast the last fifty feet before he pulled ahead to spring onto the dock in front of her. They collapsed, laughing against each other, in a heap.

"You're pretty good," he said panting. "If I'd known that—"

"I almost had you, didn't I?" Playfully, she slapped his thigh.

"You had me, all right." Grabbing her hands, Steve pulled her up. "Got your breath yet?"

"Just about—give me a minute."

Steve pulled his shirt off and threw it on the dock. His shoes and socks followed until he was wearing only a low-cut Lycra swimsuit.

"What are you doing?" Lauren's eyes widened.

"We're going swimming."

"Are you kidding? That water's cold!"

"I do it all the time."

"Maybe you do, but—"

"It's not a bridge, and it's not a hundred feet down," he coaxed. "Let's go."

Lauren kicked off her tennis shoes and jeans; then Steve grabbed her hand and they leaped off the dock into the lake.

The instant she hit the water she felt as if she had jumped into a pool of ice. The sensation was ecstatic, burning for an instant as the heat from her skin clashed with the frigid water. Then the temperature took charge and she reacted to the cold. She shot for the surface, laughing.

"Good, huh?" Facing her, Steve managed to tread water without rippling the surface.

"I love it!" she shouted. "I never thought I'd be swimming in an Alaskan lake." She had never felt more alive.

After a few minutes, she slow-kicked to the shore, following Steve's strong overhand crawl. They waded in, laughing and splashing the crystalline water at each other.

Steve brought a blanket from the cabin and carefully laid it on the sand. They stretched out beside one another to bask in the mild sunshine.

"Nice, isn't it?"

"It's wonderful," she agreed. "Where else can you swim in glacial water, lie on the beach, and there's not another human being within a hundred miles of you?"

"I know. The good points definitely outweigh the bad. I can always fly out if I want a taste of the lower forty."

That's how I've come to think of you, Buckner. The good points definitely outweigh the bad.

The late-afternoon breeze blew in a cloud cover that cloaked the sun's warming rays. Lauren retrieved her clothing and ran for the cabin.

Later that evening, she stretched out on the thick lambskin rug in front of old Ironsides. Full of rainbow trout Steve had caught, she felt totally relaxed. They had finished a game of checkers that he won soundly.

The ponderous clouds that had swept in earlier now thundered with the occasional booms and rattles of an electrical summer storm. Soon a steady, pelting rain pattered on the roof, enhancing her feeling of contentment. She felt safe from everything.

Steve brought coffee drinks laced with a cream liqueur, then joined her in front of old Ironsides. Eyeing her over the rim of his mug, he whispered, "May I be honest with you?"

All she had ever wanted from him was honesty, and now, without prompting, he was ready to level with her. "Of course, Steve. What is it?"

"You've had me in a turmoil since you arrived."

"Meaning?"

"I don't want something temporary with you," he whispered. "I want more. A commitment. I want you with me."

Lauren met his gaze with longing. "What are you saying, Steve?"

"When you're ready. I want you to come to me."

"What if I said I'm ready?"

"Not yet. We'll need some time, some distance," he managed to say.

"I've had that. These past two weeks—"

"When you get back to San Diego you'll see I'm right. If you decide to come back, we'll talk about this again."

Lauren felt disappointment paint a sad smile on her face. *Maybe he's right. When I'm back on my own turf, things might be different. Richard will probably want to begin where we left off. I always thought I would marry a man who held a degree, a man who wore suits to work, and wing-tip shoes. Wouldn't I?*

"I never thought I'd feel this way again, Lauren. Those weeks around you and away from you. It's been hard."

"I know," she murmured. "I felt the same way." She had experienced the same lack of sleep, the same longing and unfulfilled desires that she suspected he had. She had looked for his face on every dark-haired man she'd seen.

She knew how he had suffered; she had suffered too. ''I know,'' she repeated.

He lightly kissed her eyelids, brows, and lips, then rolled to his side, drawing her back against his chest.

''Someday,'' he murmured.

She nodded in agreement, unable to speak. Her emotions had risen to fever pitch, burst, and now receded slowly. He seemed loving, attentive, and sincere. She nestled into the warm circle of his arms and sighed deeply. Although she knew time was already stealing this man from her, she wished this moment could last.

Chapter Eleven

On Sunday morning Lauren sat cross-legged in front of the fire. Ironsides' belly yawned wide. The steady hum of burning wood, flames climbing high in the flue, occasional popping, and a minuscule fireworks display kept her company. Blue alcohol vapors escaped the wood, hissing as the fire devoured its prey. A noisy pop punctuated her thoughts and commanded attention to a red-orange shower of sparks.

After this summer can I really expect to go back to San Diego and pretend none of this happened? Could I ever be happy behind my desk and papers and not flying over the lakes and tundra of Alaska? Never lie in front of old Ironsides and feel Steve beside me?

The thought of leaving it all behind brought tears to her eyes. Just saying good-bye to Steve at the dock earlier— knowing their relationship would change further still with Mark's arrival—troubled her. Did he feel the loss too? How would he feel when they said good-bye permanently? There was so much they needed to talk about.

The fire settled, having burned the birch logs to skeletal red embers. To escape her blue mood, Lauren rummaged

160

through her duffel bag for a lightweight windbreaker and headed out the door.

She traced yesterday's footsteps along the shore, where they had walked together, and saw erratic prints where they had run back.

Even the birds know when it's time to fly south. Why don't I admit it's hopeless for me to stay? What's wrong with me? If I had any sense at all, I'd be on the plane tomorrow.

In the distance she heard the drone of a small aircraft. Pinpointing its direction, she watched as Steve and Mark landed in Buckner's Bay.

While Steve secured the plane, Mark bounded onto the dock.

"Lauren, how's my favorite sister?"

"Your only sister," she corrected, then hugged him. "Fine. How about you? Did you get paid?"

"Did we? Take a look at this."

Grinning broadly, Mark whipped a check from his breast pocket and waved it in front of her. Lauren unfolded the paper and examined it—a check from Naknek Cannery for $28,000, payable to Mark Cole and Lauren Cole. Lauren looked again to be sure her eyes read what they saw.

"Twenty-eight thousand? Mark—is this for real?"

"You bet it is. It was worth it, wasn't it?"

"I'll say. It's fantastic."

"We had more coming to us than we thought. Now you can set up your business, just like I promised."

Lauren pressed the check to her chest and looked in Steve's direction, but his back was turned toward them. "My share will take care of the initial lease, Mark. Thank you."

"I wouldn't have been able to fish without your help, Lauren. You worked for this as hard as I did. So when are you leaving?"

Lauren glanced in Steve's direction. "Let's talk about it later, OK?"

"Right. It's time to celebrate—starting now."

It was impossible to stay thoughtful or depressed when Mark was around. His buoyant personality had both Lauren and Steve laughing before long. Steve handed groceries through the cockpit to Mark; then Mark passed them to Lauren in a three-way relay.

The men unloaded charcoal, steaks, and a bottle of California pinot noir for their barbecue. Mark appointed himself head chef, taking charge of preparing the inch-thick T-bones in a gourmet marinade—a blend of lemon, vinegar, onion, and spices. While they waited for the charcoal, Steve's eyes met Lauren's. She glanced at Mark, but he seemed unaware of the looks passing between his partner and his twin.

When the coals were ready, Mark lifted the juicy T-bones onto the hibachi grill. The chilly afternoon air forced them inside while the meat was left to cook.

Mark let out a long sigh, looking quite pleased with himself; his innocent grin and manner had not changed in the years that separated the boy from the man. It occurred to Lauren that she envied that carefree spirit.

"You haven't changed, Mark."

"What? My clothes?" He pulled at his baggy gray trousers, then grabbed the hem of his shirt and inspected himself at different angles. "I meant to, but—"

"No, you clown. Your attitude. You still act as if you're five years old and have the world by its tail."

Mark laughed and rumpled his sister's hair affectionately. "We've had some good times, haven't we? And you've gotten me out of a few scrapes here and there."

Lauren nodded.

"I guess you'll just have to come with me, Lauren. Keep me out of trouble. Next stop, Hawaii! September will see me tanning to a deep golden brown, wearing nothing but my heathen skin, sipping mai tais under a swaying palm tree.''

''Sounds good to me,'' Steve agreed.

''Me too,'' Lauren chimed. ''I wish I could go.''

''You can both go. Just pack your bags and come along.''

''That may work for you, Mark. But I've had enough adventure to last me awhile.'' Lauren avoided the gaze from Steve's smoky gray eyes.

''That's the trouble with you, Lauren. You're too dependable, too levelheaded.''

''And you're too wild and unpredictable.''

''You said she was your little sister, Mark. You didn't tell me you were twins.''

''She is my little sister, technically. I was born before midnight on April first; she was born on April second.''

''He was an April fool,'' Lauren said. ''I was born four minutes later, and he's never let me forget it!''

''You're so different, I would've never believed it.'' Steve shook his head. ''I pity your poor parents.''

''And the teachers, and the doctors, and the police.'' Mark laughed.

''Speaking of which,'' Lauren chimed in, ''did you two finish your business with the authorities?''

''After the police threatened Marin with murder charges against the brothers, he agreed to cooperate. He had evidence that Randy had been paying him off over the past year. Sherry had orchestrated it and set it up between them, apparently. What a nightmare.'' Steve sipped his wine. ''I never would have believed Randy was involved.''

''What will happen to them?'' Lauren asked.

''Randy and Marin have been arrested. Sherry's out on bail—''

"Thanks to her dad," Mark added. "I can't believe he's still doing it."

Lauren felt ashamed that she had suspected Steve—remembering how determined she had been trying to prove that he was the mastermind behind Mark's troubles.

"I have a confession to make, Steve."

Steve looked wary. "What?"

"Just a minute." Lauren left their company and rifled through her bag to produce his personal ledger and Mark's folder.

"Where'd you get those?"

"Borrowed them from your office," she said simply. "I hope you'll forgive me."

"I thought I'd lost them."

"You're not angry?"

"No."

"Thank God they weren't in the office," Mark said. "Sherry destroyed everything that would implicate her."

"This should prove Johnson's claim," Steve said, finding the entry he sought. "There. See that?"

He showed Lauren the amount due Johnson. "From what we could determine, Sherry deducted about twenty percent of that before he got paid. I suspect everyone else got the same treatment. Including you, Mark."

Mark shook his head. "Sherry altered the books and skimmed a share for herself. What do they call that?"

"Embezzling," Lauren stated.

"She was clever, all right," Mark jeered.

Sharp *was the description I heard.* "Did they actually kill those boys?" Lauren asked.

"The police believe it was an accident. They were independent of my operation and not a target. That's all I know."

Lauren breathed a sigh of relief, and the room became silent for a moment.

''I guess I'll go check on our steaks,'' Mark said, leaping to his feet. ''Be right back.''

''I have something for you, Lauren,'' Steve said, looking sheepish.

''You do?''

He leaned back, working his hand into the small front pocket of his jeans, and drew out a slender gold chain.

''For me?'' Steve dropped it into her open palm. ''It's beautiful, Steve.'' She began to fasten it around her neck.

''You don't mind, do you? I mean—I thought maybe you'd wear your grandmother's ring on it.''

She stopped before she had connected the clasp behind her neck. Lauren walked across the room to where her duffel bag lay beside the bunk, and extracted her ring from a zippered jewelry bag. She slipped it over one end of the chain, fastened the clasp, then slipped the necklace over her head. The ring lay nestled in the valley between her breasts.

''Thank you, Steve.''

I'm sorry I acted so . . .'' He paused.

''Jealous?'' she suggested.

''Well . . .''

Lauren smiled.

''You'll accept my peace offering then?'' he asked.

''It's lovely, Steve. I'll cherish it.'' *And you, forever.*

''Lauren, don't leave'' was all it would take for her to change her mind. But that was not to be. She touched the unruly curl that lay on his forehead; faint dimples disappeared into the well-groomed beard. The spell broke when Mark clambered up the stairs and into the cabin. Lauren dropped her hand.

''Steaks are doing fine. They're almost ready.'' Mark seated himself again, then asked, ''What are your plans, Steve? Are you heading south for the winter?''

Steve stared into the flames of the potbellied stove as he

answered, "After I get this mess settled, I think I'll take some time off. I've got to work out the details with Mallory and my attorney in Anchorage. I don't know how long that will take, but I'll be back on Friday."

"Is Sherry going to jail?" Lauren asked.

Steve shifted his weight. "We'll definitely go to trial."

"Marin?"

"He's in jail, awaiting trial right now. He had outstanding warrants in Juneau and a police record in Ketchikan."

"You were dealing with real criminals!" Lauren shook her head.

"Well, when this is over I thought I might fly the Mooney to San Diego for Christmas, stay a couple of weeks or so. Would you mind playing tour guide for a while, Lauren?"

"He'd love Old Town at Christmas, wouldn't he?" Mark suggested.

"Let her think about it, Mark. I can't reason on an empty stomach. I doubt if she can. Have you burned our meat bad enough yet?"

"Coming right up." Mark shot out the door again.

"I thought I'd rent an apartment while I was there." Steve's pleasant baritone sent ripples across the air for Lauren to embrace.

"Not if you're coming to see me, you won't. I have an extra bedroom." Lauren gently trailed her fingers over his cheek to his beard, then outlined his lips with the tip of her finger. His face remained impenetrable, as it had been all evening. He leaned toward her and stole a kiss.

When Mark reentered the cabin, he presented the tray of steaks like Jean-Pierre at the Inn. A terry-cloth hand towel was draped over his left arm, and the barbecue fork was poised in the air as he waited for Steve to decide which one would be his.

"And you, mademoiselle?"

Lauren chose the smaller of the two remaining steaks, although each weighed at least a pound.

Mark then retrieved the red wine and opened it with an ostentatious pop. ''The finest red wine in Dillingham, monsieur—next to Old Man Brand's chokecherry punch, that is—*très bon*?''

Steve swirled the wine in the chipped mug, sniffed the bouquet, then held a small sample in his mouth as though making a serious appraisal. ''Yes. I think that will do. It's got good body. I like a wine with legs.''

''A fine wine is like a lovely woman,'' Mark lectured in a phony French accent. ''It must breathe and it must have legs.''

''Come on, you two.'' Lauren laughed. ''Let's eat before our food gets cold.''

The remainder of the evening passed quickly. Steve stoked Ironsides a couple of times before Lauren stretched and yawned.

''Well, I guess I'm going to bed. It's been nice. Thank you, both.'' She kissed Mark on the forehead.

''I'm going out for some fresh air,'' Mark said, rising. ''Then I'm going to turn in too.''

''Want a lantern?'' Steve pointed at the squat green Coleman that sat on the counter.

''Yeah. I'll take it.''

''Okay.'' Steve chuckled. ''That female brown's been hanging around. She was acting pretty lonely when I saw her last.''

''If I'm not back in ten minutes, follow the bear tracks.''

The heavy door swung shut and they were finally alone.

Steve rose from the stump chair and pulled Lauren to him. ''Can you forgive me? I've been such a jerk.''

''I thought that was my line, Steve. It'll all be over soon, right?''

''As soon as I'm through in Anchorage, it'll be over.''

Lauren's body stiffened slightly and her breath caught in her throat. She hoped Steve wouldn't be subject to any more of the Mallory/Marin/Scott brand of business. Hopefully, Steve's lawyer would see to that. She wound her fingers into his thick hair and gently guided him to her. She kissed him as though it would be their last time.

Steve groaned softly. ''Good night, Lauren.''

Steve joined Mark outside while Lauren removed her shoes and jeans, then crawled under the covers. She burrowed her head deep into the downy fluff. Wrapping her arms around herself, she began to dream about an enigmatic pirate. She drifted to sleep, lulled by their muffled conversation and the comforting heat that emanated from old Ironsides.

On Monday morning the trio flew from their private paradise back to Dillingham and reality. The two precious days that Lauren had shared with Steve had completed her metamorphosis from the unsure, scared girl back to the self-assured, confident woman she knew herself to be.

They parted at the airport, Steve driving the fleet van into town, so Mark and Lauren drove ahead into the bustling postseason fishing village.

Jostling in her brother's antiquated Jeep over bumps and potholes in the gravel road, Lauren remembered her first ride into Dillingham—it felt like years ago. Only now the meadow seemed even greener, the sky was clear, and, although her mind was preoccupied with thoughts of Steve Buckner, they were more kindly than the first time she traveled that road.

She wouldn't feel that Steve was completely free of the problems until all this business had been resolved and he returned triumphant. Lauren didn't question, nor did she understand, why Steve chose to keep their relationship a secret. He wouldn't acknowledge it even to Mark, who ap-

collateral is tied up in the property, and he's lost just about everything.''

''Oh, my,'' Lauren said sympathetically. ''He seemed like such a sweet kid.''

''I think he was; that's the hard part. I don't know how deeply he was involved except through money. From what Steven said, Sherry seems to have masterminded this mess.''

''And Marin?''

''The lawyers are sure he will spend time in jail. We don't know yet what will happen to Sherry.''

''Emily, that's awful. It's hard to believe. And what's really scary is that Mark and I were in the middle of it. He had a feeling something bad was going on, but I guess none of us knew to what degree.''

''Yes. Steven's pretty shook up. I don't know how long this will go on.''

''Did he have anything else to say?'' Lauren asked.

''Well, Steven has offered to let me take over the lodge. He's selling it to me for his share of the damages he incurred, and I will take it over. I couldn't have planned, dreamed, or wished for anything so grand.''

''Emily, that's wonderful news! How exciting!''

Emily lifted a corner of her apron to her eyes. ''It's a dream come true, dear. But that's Steven. He's been so good to me throughout the years. Better than I deserve.''

Lauren hugged the older woman, and for a moment they simply held each other.

''Emily, that's so wonderful. I'm so happy for you.''

''I'd wish the same for you, Lauren. Steven is a wonderful man, and if you wanted to, you two could be very happy.''

''What am I going to do? I can't just camp out on his doorstep. And I don't want to leave here with a broken heart.''

Richard's letter, the only one she had received from him all summer, held terms and proposals that simply didn't interest her. She knew the two of them had no future.

"It seems so impossible," Lauren said thoughtfully. "I had no intention of staying when I came here. Now nothing seems to matter except being with Steve."

Emily reflected on the younger woman's words for a moment before answering.

"You know, Lauren, I was a lot like you when I came here nigh fifty years ago. I answered an ad from the only doctor in town at the time and came up to be his nurse. I was single, scared, and it was a mean feat to get here in those days.

"I booked northern passage from San Francisco on a steamer that took so long I thought we were headed for China. When we finally made port in Anchorage, I found my way to a little airstrip that was smaller than ours here in Dillingham, mind you. And I found Max. He was a swaggerin', quiet sort of man who stole my heart while we flew over those ranges in that little prop plane of his.

"The only difference I can see is, Max had me engaged to him before the summer was out and we were married soon after."

"It almost sounds like the stuff dreams are made of," Lauren said.

"Well, over the years I've wasted a lot of time ignoring my dreams. I had loads of excuses. I told myself I was too old, it wasn't practical, it was too risky, too whatever. But you know"—Emily sighed—"when you take a look at your life and realize you have only so much time to spend, doesn't it make sense to do what you really want to do? I miss my Max terribly, but I wouldn't trade all of our memories for the world. Let fate play a hand in this, Lauren. Seems that it already has."

Lauren hadn't thought about it in such simple terms before. Her career in accounting had been a means of supporting herself, but it did not have to be the focal point of her life.

"If Steven's the man you love, you've got to tell him and risk the consequences. If I've ever seen a man in love, it's him. But either way, honesty is the best course to take."

Isn't that exactly what I've been demanding of him? Lauren thought shamefully. *His lack of communication drove me to think he was dishonest and disreputable most of the summer.*

"I've got a few days to think about it, Emily. Steve should be back Friday."

"Pity's sake, Lauren. Tell him how you feel. If I know Steven, he won't say anything on his own. You may have to encourage him a little."

Lauren considered the long, lonely months that she would spend in San Diego separated from Steve. He seemed to think they needed the time alone to be objective about their relationship. Maybe he was right—maybe time was the answer. She would encourage him to visit at Christmas. Until then, she could lose herself in her work.

Lauren hugged the older woman. Sugar and spice scented the pillowy embrace she had grown to love. "I'll think about it, Emily. Thank you so much. And I'm so happy for you."

"Thank you, dear. You rest well. We'll talk again tomorrow."

Pleasantly tired, Lauren descended the narrow stairs and headed toward the confines of her tiny room. The more she contemplated the idea of residing in Dillingham, the more feasible it seemed. But, Lauren reasoned, Steve might assume that she was after his assets and his name. It would seem as if she were husband hunting after all.

As Lauren entered the lobby, Mark bounded through the hallway, whooped boisterously, and said, "Come on, Lauren. We're going out!"

Chapter Twelve

Dressed in sandals, shorts, and an outrageous red, purple, and yellow print shirt that fluttered like loose feathers as he danced around her, Mark looked to Lauren like a floundering exotic bird that crash-landed on the wrong shore.

He grabbed her hand and tugged her toward the door.

"Wait a minute. I'm not dressed to go out," Lauren objected. "I've been in the kitchen all day."

"You look great. We're only going to the tavern."

"All right. I want to talk with you, but let me change my blouse, at least."

"Hurry up." Mark danced around her, imitating his island brothers. "Night's a wastin'."

Lauren hurried to her room, threw off her work shirt, and snatched a clean knit blouse and slipped it on. A few minutes later, the twins entered the dark, noisy tavern.

Someone whistled for the waitress, and another patron called out to a friend from one of the small round tables across the room. A few men stood around the single pool table, watching a closely matched game. Cigarette smoke swirled around their heads in large, snaky patterns.

"What'll you have, stranger?" A heavily painted waitress sidled up to their table; she balanced the plastic serving tray within her arm like a barroom veteran and trained her eyes on Mark.

"Are you ready to order, or do I have to come back?"

"I'm ready," Mark answered. "How about you, Lauren?"

"Well, I—"

"Hey, darlin' . . . we're getting a little dry over here."

Lauren's eyes followed the voice to a man in the corner. She saw a red-cheeked, russet-haired customer waving an empty bottle at the waitress.

"Be right there, Mallory." Turning to Mark and Lauren, she said, "Go ahead, you two. What do you want?"

"Mallory?" Lauren repeated.

"Yeah. Since Sherry's been gone, he's been here every day this week. A real pain in my behind. She's in Anchorage settling her business with Buckner."

"But—" Lauren's throat constricted and she began coughing. Her eyes widened in panic, fixing on her brother.

"I'll have a beer," Mark said, lifting one finger. "Gonna be OK, Lauren? What do you want?"

Covering her mouth, Lauren shook her head. "Water," she squeaked, and covered again.

Mark held two fingers in a *V* sign and said, "Make that two beers and a water."

"You got it." Heading back toward the bar, the waitress swayed her hips, emphasizing the tightness of her bulging jeans.

"Mark, did you hear what she said?" Lauren rasped.

"Yeah. So what?"

"Steve's going to be gone all week," Lauren explained. "With Sherry."

"So. What's the big deal?" her brother asked nonchalantly.

Her ultimate fear engulfed her. Steve had lied to her. Mark seemed oblivious to his sister's distress. She had fallen in love with his friend—his partner—and Steve had lied to her. She couldn't confide in Mark—couldn't estrange him now when she had no choice but to leave. And she would leave. Right away.

The painted waitress returned with two bottles of beer, a glass of water, and a baiting smile intended for Mark. The dollar tip he added to the bill lit her face as she expertly folded it and tucked it into a revealing neckline.

"Thanks, hon," she said, grinning. "I'll check back with you in a while."

"Come on, darlin'," Mallory called again.

"Coming, Red," the waitress hollered. "Keep your shirt on."

Lauren reached for the water and drank deeply, as though she were dousing a fire, allowing the cool liquid to soothe and relax the tight cords in her throat. When she could finally speak she asked, "Does she know I'm your sister, or is she always that brazen?" Lauren's eyes narrowed on the retreating figure.

"She knows how to get along in a place like this. So . . . are you planning to fly out this weekend or wait for me?"

Lauren cleared her throat. "I've decided that if I can get a flight out, I'll leave tomorrow."

"Tomorrow? I thought you'd at least stay the weekend. Steve's coming back on Frid—"

"Tomorrow," she repeated.

"Well, if that's what you want. . . . I sure hate to see you go."

"I know, Mark. It's been great being with you. I didn't realize how much I missed you until this summer. It's going to be pretty lonely when I get back."

"Sure you don't want to forget San Diego? You could

come to Hawaii with me.'' He grabbed the front of his Hawaiian shirt and shook it.

''No. I've got a contract to sign and a business to start. That's what I really want to do. Until then, I never will be independent. I've stayed longer than I should have already.''

''And I guess Richard's waiting for you too, huh?''

Lauren didn't respond.

''I suppose you're right,'' Mark conceded. ''But Steve'll be disappointed.''

I'm sure he'll manage. Lauren felt her face tighten as she set the half-finished water glass on the table. ''I'm going to bed, Mark. Are you going to stay a while?''

''Yeah. If you're going to leave tomorrow, I will too. I'll be in later. Don't wait up for me.''

Lauren was glad her brother didn't insist on walking her back to their shared room. She felt relieved she'd have privacy to dwell on her hurt feelings alone.

She marched back to the hotel through the evening fog of heavy, moist air. Wetness pricked her flushed cheeks and formed tiny droplets of water on her face. Sadness grew into a lump that lay heavy in her stomach. She felt sick. Her thoughts about staying in Dillingham were irretrievably lost.

If Buckner could lie about his business dealings, he'd lie about other things as well. He had finally done it—proven what she had suspected and didn't want to believe. She couldn't trust him.

The door to the lobby boomed when it shut behind her, leaving her in the empty, dimly lit foyer alone. Her footsteps echoed as she walked, and it seemed the noise of fitting the key into the lock reverberated through the hallway. Everything seemed larger than it should be, as if she were in a dream where size and emotions were exaggerated beyond the real.

Every surge from her heart drummed mercilessly in her head and amplified her pain. Her skin stung from the salty flow of tears that had dried in the hollows beneath her eyes. It was late when she fell asleep—later still when Mark tiptoed into their room.

The next day, Lauren telephoned reservations for the commercial flight to Anchorage. She dressed like other northern travelers this time, in her jeans, boots, and jacket.

It was hard enough to leave her heart behind; but she couldn't face the man who had thrown it away. Saying good-bye to Emily was difficult. Emily gathered Lauren in her arms and pressed her close.

"Life is full of the most beautiful people, Lauren. You're one of them who makes it worthwhile to me. I don't want to see you go," she said sniffing. "I wish there was something more I could do or say, but I understand. Take care of yourself, now. And don't forget that I love you."

"I won't, Emily." Lauren squeezed her friend again, blinking back the tears that stood in her eyes.

"You're going too, Mark?" Emily wiped her eyes with her apron.

"Yeah." He threw his sister's baggage into the Jeep and reluctantly climbed behind the wheel. "See you in May, Emmie—if I'm not back before then. I'll leave the Jeep keys at the hangar."

"I'll let Steven know. Now don't forget that pineapple you promised me."

"I can already taste that cheesecake," he teased. "Pineapple oozing over the side . . ."

Lauren waved as they drove away and watched as their friend grew smaller in the distance. Steve's words came back to haunt her: *Once you've seen Alaska, you never go all the way home . . .* Her throat burned as though a heavy hand held on, intent to squeeze the life from it; her heart threatened to burst the steel cage that held it tight. She thought she was through with crying last night, but it wasn't true.

Finally she turned to her brother and said, ''You didn't have to go with me, Mark.''

''Why not?'' He cupped his hand behind his ear. ''The islands are calling. I can hear them already.''

Leave it to Mark to make a joke when my heart's been torn in two.

''I thought I'd go as far as Anchorage with you. It's the least I can do for my partner.''

At Dillingham's one-room airport, they checked in at the only ticket counter and had their baggage flagged with the appropriate tag that read ANC. It would be a twenty-minute wait, as the flight had been delayed from Anchorage.

Lauren tucked her hands into her jacket pocket and stood outside the Dillingham Air office, while Mark paced back and forth like an impatient traveler, checking his watch and scanning the sky for the plane that wasn't there.

''It'll be here soon, Mark. Maybe that's it now.'' Lauren pointed in the direction of an approaching airplane, a steady drone growing in volume.

''Yeah.'' Mark's face altered from an anxious frown to a slight smile. ''I think you're right.''

Lauren shielded her eyes to focus more clearly on the growing shape. Her pulse raced as the plane came into view. She almost expected Buckner's Mooney to appear, but it was the commercial jet that landed with the noise of a rocket blast—not the gleaming Mooney. With a heavy heart, she followed her brother up the outdoor ramp and into the crowded commuter plane that would take them to Anchorage.

Once inside the International Airport, Mark waited with Lauren in the long line at the Alaskan Airlines counter. She searched his face for the excitement she presumed would be there, but his exuberance was masked behind a troubled exterior of little-boy rejection. His shoulders bowed with sorrow that Lauren well remembered, like when he'd lost a baseball game or his current best friend.

"I loved being with you, Mark. I'm glad everything turned out well for you."

Mark's lips curved into a small, sad smile. "You going to marry puddin' face?"

"I don't think I will, Mark. I can't believe I ever considered it." She toyed with the ring that hung from the chain around her neck and tried not to cry. "Come see me in San Diego, will you? You know where I live." She gave him a squeeze, then moved up to the front of the counter when the attendant said, "Next."

After her bags were tossed onto the conveyer belt, Mark handed the cosmetics case to her.

"You're all set, Lauren. Take care of yourself."

"Right," she answered stoically. "Have fun in Sun Land."

"No doubt. I have to check the standby status for the next flight out." He pecked her on the cheek and hooked his thumb into the shoulder strap of his heavy weekend bag; everything he owned he had stuffed into the small leather satchel. "I'll send you a postcard." He waved good-bye, then made an abrupt about-face and ambled away.

Lauren thought Mark seemed suddenly eager to leave her and be on his way. When he had gotten about twenty feet, Lauren impulsively shouted, "Mark, wait. Come back here."

He returned with a surprised look on his face.

"I need to tell you something," she said, furrowing the line on her face.

"What's that?"

"You're not really my twin, you know. The milkman

brought you.'' The shocked expression that replaced the curious look on his face broke Lauren into a fit of laughter. ''Gotcha.'' Mark laughed good-naturedly. It was the first time Lauren had ever done anything like it. It felt good. She watched as he ambled down the concourse and disappeared.

Alone again, Lauren forged a path through the mobs of people headed toward her boarding area. Fortunately, she wouldn't have much of a wait; her plane would be leaving shortly.

When she reached her gate, her mind seemed dull and dazed, not unlike her first time in the same airport. Her boarding gate was one of the last on the concourse and in the middle of the hustle and bustle of the hordes of stateside fishermen returning home. Her thoughts exploded like a bursting balloon as she heard her name announced over the intercom.

''Lauren Cole, Miss Lauren Cole, please come to a white paging telephone.''

''Now what?'' *Mark would never let me pull one over on him and get away with it,* she decided. She scanned the corridor and found a courtesy phone perched on a stanchion. She picked up the receiver and heard the familiar buzzing tone, then a click.

''Lauren Cole here.''

''Please return to the Alaskan Airlines ticket counter.''

''My bro—'' A click abruptly ended her question before she could ask. She looked at the handset she gripped in her hand, wishing it were the neck of the rude operator.

Lauren checked her purse for her ticket, just to be certain she had it. When she didn't see it, she frantically patted her jacket, her jeans—front and back—and tore into her purse again. It wasn't there.

She shifted the straps of her purse, clutched her cosmetics case, and jogged down the concourse. Weaving and dodging through the crowd, like a running back headed for the end zone, she prayed she wouldn't miss her flight.

This wouldn't have happened if you'd been thinking straight, she scolded herself.

Going against the flow of human traffic, Lauren used her arm as a shield against the jostling she was getting.

Panting heavily, she reached the ticket area and stepped through the line to the front of the counter. There, leaning against the booth, a tall, rugged-looking man dressed in faded denims and a wool plaid shirt, hands tucked inside a red down vest, grinned at her from behind his mirror-lensed sunglasses.

"Buckner!" Her loud cry burst without restraint, and a whole line of eyes turned in Lauren's direction.

"Looking for someone?"

"Definitely not you."

"This must déjà vu." He removed his glasses and grinned, devilment flashing in his pale gray eyes. "I feel like I've been here before. . . . Excuse us, folks." His wide smile and long arm cut a path through the line, as he moved Lauren away from the curious travelers.

"But I was called back. I think I left my—"

He fanned an airline ticket in front of her. "Your ticket?"

"Yes," she said quietly, lowering her eyes to the ticket folder he held.

"Not like you to run off and leave something behind, is it?"

His question was weighted with words unspoken, and Lauren felt an aching heaviness in her throat. Tears formed and stood in her eyes as she tried to avoid his.

"Were you in such a hurry that you couldn't say good-bye?"

"I had to get back to San Diego. Back where I belong."

Steve froze. His handsome, bearded face looked confused, angry, hurt. "But what about us? I thought—"

Lauren's pent-up emotions spilled like an overfilled dam. "Us?" There's never been *us*. I can't trust a man who lies to me."

"What are you talking about?"

"Mallory. He's been in Dillingham all week, not in Anchorage with you. But Sherry was."

Steve's narrowed brows and frowning lips seemed carved in granite as Lauren confronted him.

"I thought I could live in Dillingham. Open my business there. I must have been crazy. I was willing to love you without conditions. For what? A man who can't be trusted? I'm only thankful I found out in time," she finished angrily.

Steve pinned Lauren with an intent glare. "I didn't lie to you, Lauren. I had to settle with Mallory like I told you, but I worked through my lawyer. Sherry's trial has been set, and we're going to court in September. I don't know where she's gone, and I don't care."

His words extinguished her emotional fire and robbed her of her anger. She looked for gray eyes to steady her as she struggled to make sense of what he had said.

Steve's voice strained with emotions he fought to control. "When Mark called me last night, I was furious with you. I felt betrayed. Sherry, Randy, Marin, then you. After all we've been through, you were walking out on me. There was no way I was going to let that happen. I finished our business this afternoon. The three of them are out of the way, for now."

"Steve, I'm so sorry. I wouldn't blame you for hating me."

Drawing her close, Steve reassured her. "I don't hate you. I love you. I'm glad you found out before it was too late. I wouldn't want any partner of mine to distrust me."

"Partner?"

Boyish dimples creased his face and banished the fierceness he'd worn just seconds before. He released her and took from his breast pocket a sheaf of papers and handed them to her.

Lauren unfolded an official quitclaim deed from Randy Scott to Mark Cole, Lauren Cole, and Steven B. Buckner for the Minnow.

"How would you like to join us? A three-way partnership?"

"You mean go into the fishing business with you?" she asked, wiping tears from her eyes.

"Well, you could say that. I don't think you'd have to be on the water, unless you wanted to, but we need a good accountant. What d'ya think?"

"I don't know. I—" Her thoughtful expression changed to one of alarm. "Randy's Minnow! Mark! We've got to find him. He's on his way—"

"Someone call?" Mark's grinning face appeared. The two men shook hands. "Darn, Steve. I thought you'd never get here."

She looked first at her brother, then back to Steve. "What is it with you two? Is this some sort of conspiracy?"

The two partners laughed.

"Getting you two together has been the hardest job I've ever had," Mark said, wiping his brow.

"Are you telling me this has been a setup?" Lauren demanded.

"Well . . ." Mark backed up, out of his sister's reach. "You know, Lauren, sometimes older brothers have to step in when sisters need a little guidance, and—"

"Don't believe it, Lauren. I love you." Steve kissed her. "And I'm going to have a lot of fun proving it to you," he whispered. "Over and over." Steve dug in his pocket and produced a small brown velvet box, which he opened as he handed it to her. ''Right after we're married.''

A heart-shaped emerald surrounded by diamonds flashed from its white satin nest. Her eyes traveled from the gold-encased emerald to his silver eyes and back again. ''You mean—''

''I want to marry you, Lauren. I want you to stay with me.''

Lauren raised her eyes to look into the face of the man who had captured her heart and soul. He looked every bit the pirate she imagined him to be.

She became oblivious to everyone and everything around her except the faint smell of spruce on his wool shirt and the rapid beating of her heart. She wanted to stay locked in his arms, sheltered from the outside within that protective, possessive circle.

''I missed you, Lauren. I could hardly stand to be away from you these past four days. I couldn't sleep last night— hoping I'd find you, afraid I'd lose you.''

Her tears stained his vest a darker shade of red where they fell. She tried to wipe them off, but they had already soaked in, and more streamed down her cheeks. Lauren wiped her eyes with her sleeve before Steve pulled his handkerchief out and handed it to her.

He took the ring from its case and slipped it onto her finger. ''Lauren, I want you to know I have no secrets, no hidden affairs, and from now on ours is going public.''

Gently, she curved her hand around the back of his head and guided him to her waiting lips. Although people stared as they detoured around them, Steve made her ignore their audience.

''Whoo-wee!'' Mark crowed, and slapped his friend on the back.

''Aren't you on your way to Hawaii or somewhere?'' Lauren asked.

"And miss my favorite sister's wedding? No way."

She leveled an accusing glare at him. "You didn't happen to pickpocket your own sister's ticket, did you?"

"I wasn't about to let you go without seeing Steve. Like I said, it's the least I could do for my partner."

"My bags!"

Mark's eyes gleamed. "They're holding them downstairs. I'll pick them up on our way out."

"I think I've been had." She eyed her new partners suspiciously, first one, then the other. "I can see right now I'm going to have to keep a tight rein on you two."

"Count on it," they replied in unison.

Lauren opened her arms to hug them both.

"What do you think about my little sister now, Steve?"

Steve's gaze shifted from Lauren's radiant face and wandered down to her boots and back again. The thoughts behind his smile were transparent to the woman he appraised.

"I don't know." Buckner tugged her T-shirt. "She's a little skinny, but I think I can take care of that."

"All right!" Mark shouted, and the two friends slapped hands, palm-to-palm, above their heads.

"Come on, L. C.," Steve said, picking up her cosmetics case. "Let's go home. There's this little place I know of . . ."

Buckner grinned wickedly as he guided Lauren out of the International Airport.

She knew without asking that they were on their way to Merrill Field, back to Dillingham, and from there . . .